THE LEPER AND THE ANGEL

By Gary

For Christine, Ben, Jamie and Alex.
Always.

Table of contents

CHAPTER 1

"Then the angel showed me the river of the water of life, as clear as crystal, flowing from the throne of God"
Revelations 22:1

It may have been a grain of hope in a desert of despair but all journeys begin with that first step.

Helmand Province, Southern Afghanistan, August 2006.

The relentless sun beat down from an azure sky. Cloaked in the shimmering heat, ancient mud walls rose up from the desert landscape like the remains of a giant pockmarked sandcastle. But there was no sign of water to wash the crumbling defences away. This was a land of hard-core summer heat, almost volcanic in its intensity. It was if an elemental subterranean force was surging from the bowels of the earth and threatening to consume everything in its wake.

A British Army Outpost stood in the middle of this boiling cauldron. More redoubt than fortification, it seemed that history could be repeating itself. 'The Siege of Lucknow', 'Rorke's Drift' – take your pick.

Sandbags and heavily armed lookout towers fortified the primitive encampment. As sweltering soldiers milled about the sandy courtyard in full combat gear, a ragged Union Jack flag fluttered defiantly above the compound.

Lieutenant Charlotte (Charly) Stevens, British Army language specialist, marched past her men as she headed for the Operations room. The grizzled squaddies exchanged cheeky smirks as the muscled twenty-something amazon powered along. The only thing missing was a sexist wolf whistle but they wouldn't dare. Some things were more lethal than a bullet.

Major Donaldson, army officer since birth, stood in the sand-infested Operations room and gazed down at a large map unfurled across a canvas table. There was a tap on the tin door and his imperious head sprung up. 'Come,' he barked.

Charly marched in and snapped to attention. Facing her commanding officer, she stood rod-straight – her blonde hair fixed up in a bun as tight as her clenched fists. The Major targeted Charly with his usual commanding glare. Eye contact at all costs. Not so much a trick picked up at Public School, but just ingrained in his DNA. You wouldn't want to shake hands with this fucker.

The Major's Etonian voice boomed within the glorified tent. 'Captain Borthwick is indisposed. Bloody lurgi. I need you to speak with that village elder and confirm that they're Taliban-free.'

'Yes sir!' bawled Charly.

The Major continued. 'Get him on side. School, medical aid, clean water supply. Whatever it takes. Report back to me at seventeen-hundred hours. That's all.'

Charly stomped to attention and saluted. 'Yes sir!'

An afterthought from the Major. 'And Lieutenant Stevens?'

'Yes sir!'

'Don't get killed. Too much bloody paperwork.'

'No sir!'

Charly wheeled round and marched out.

A solitary British Army 'Snatch' Land Rover churned through the dust of a remote dirt track. In the rear of the buffeted vehicle, Charly sat perspiring in full combat gear. Two sweat-drenched infantrymen sat opposite their charge. One of the heavily armed squaddies glanced at Charly then turned to his comrade. 'What a fucking joke,' he whispered.

On an elevated ridge, further up the track, an ambush party of Taliban warriors lay flat on their bellies. Their uniform was basic; biblical beards, turbans and billowing tunics enveloped by ammunition vests.

Khalid, the intense commander, waited with an RPG launcher tucked into his shoulder. Although only in his late twenties, he appeared ageless – like the rocky terrain which supported his prostrate body. His piercing eyes narrowed as he focussed intently on the approaching vehicle.

In the front of the Land Rover, the army driver peered through the dirt-encrusted windscreen. His eyes blinked and strained with the incessant glare of the Afghanistan sun. He leaned forward and squinted as a shaft of light bounced off something metallic at the side of the road. Then he spotted it - the barrel of a RPG launcher pointing directly towards him. 'RPG!' he screamed to his passengers in the back.

Khalid unleashed the rocket. It scythed through the air, leaving a portentous smoke trail in its wake, and slammed into the side of the Land Rover. An orange fireball engulfed the vehicle as it keeled onto its side and careered along the dirt.

After a few chaotic seconds, the dust and smoke began to clear and the devastation was revealed. Bodies, and body parts, littered the ground around the burning wreckage.

On the ridge, the Taliban group chanted in celebration. 'Allahu Akbar! Allahu Akbar!'

A mutilated army soldier writhed in the scorched earth beside the smouldering vehicle. Salim, the Taliban sniper, fixed his telescopic sight on his victim's charred face. Crack! The soldier's body jerked like a doll and became still.

A second soldier lay screaming in agony on the ground. Skin and sinew flapped around the bloody stumps where his legs had been only thirty seconds before. Salim fired again.

A dazed figure emerged from the mangled wreckage. It was Charly. Salim instantly spotted her and took careful aim. Through his scope he could see a blonde-haired woman in a torn soldier's uniform. Her right cheek was ripped open and streaming blood.

Charly staggered towards the critically injured driver . His twisted body lay fatally exposed in the open but he was moaning so she knew he stood a chance. Salim targeted Charly's chest. His trigger finger hovered but didn't squeeze. Charly began to drag the barely conscious man towards the rear of the shattered Land Rover. Salim followed her with his telescopic sight but still he didn't fire. Something was holding him back.

'Salim!' Khalid screamed in Arabic. 'Do it!'

But the moment was lost. Charly and the driver disappeared behind the wreckage.

Khalid's men jumped to their feet in celebration. They raked the remains of the despoiled Land Rover with their AK47s. The charred metal sang with the ricocheting bullets as the jubilant Arabs advanced towards their prize.

Then a staccato crackling filled the suffocating air as Charly reappeared from behind the wreckage, firing a light machine gun from her hip. A lethal hail of bullets tore into the advancing Taliban. Four Arabs fell instantly. Khalid crumpled to the ground, blood streaming from his left eye. Charly continued to advance and fire like an avenging automaton. 'Come on you bastards! Come on!' she screamed.

The whirr of approaching rotor blades sounded in the sky.

Salim looked up and recognized the imminent danger. 'Apache! Take cover. Now!' he shouted.

Dodging Charly's blizzard of bullets, Salim grabbed his injured commander and called across to his comrade, Jamal. 'Take Khalid's arm.' As the two men dragged a semi-conscious Khalid to safety, Salim grinned at Jamal. 'She's a crazy woman.'

Charly sneered as she watched the Taliban abandon their fallen comrades and sprint away. She halted, ceased fire then backtracked, covering her own retreat. As she passed the dead and wounded Arabic fighters she riddled them with bullets. Just to be sure. Until nothing moved but her trigger finger.

Then a stumble. Charly lurched forward and seemed to freeze for a moment. The machine gun dropped from her grasp. Her limbs stiffened and her vacant eyes rolled back into her head. She crumpled to the ground, foaming at the mouth. Charly jerked and shook like a rag doll as a major convulsive seizure overwhelmed her.

The chopping of the rotor blades increased in volume and dust whirled around the jolting figure as a metal angel descended from the sky.

CHAPTER 2

Yemen, 2011.

A crackling fire glowed and sparked in the chilled night air. It marked the burning heart of a primitive campsite, situated beside the entrance to a mountain cave. It looked like anytime within the last two thousand years. Only the AK47 resting against a boulder signalled modernity.

The leper squatted alone in the shadows by the fire. Like an unearthly apparition, he was swaddled in cloth from head to foot. His intense eyes were the only features visible as he stared hypnotically into the dancing flames.

As tiny pieces of ash swirled in the smoky gloom, the leper sang quietly to himself in Arabic. A beautiful and plaintive Yemeni folk song floated up into the clear night sky.

A screech penetrated the enveloping darkness. The leper's head jerked up. Remaining as still as an Egyptian mummy, he listened. Silence again. He relaxed. His claw-like hand stretched across the flames and tore a piece of meat from the small carcass roasting over the fire. He stuffed the morsel underneath the cloth covering his deformed face and started to chew.

***

London, 2011.

A single bed in a darkened room. Charly's fumbling hand emerged from underneath a quilt and eventually battered the beeping alarm clock into submission.

Her eyes fluttered open. She rolled to the side of her mattress, sat up and yawned. Reaching across to a side table, she grabbed a foil of capsules and swallowed two with a slug of water.

Charly leaned on her elbow for a few seconds, waiting for the synapses to start firing in her brain.

Ready.

In one fluid movement, she fell to the hardwood floor. Her hands slapped on the smooth surface as she commenced a punishing series of push-ups. Usual routine to greet the day.

Dripping with sweat, Charly padded naked into her gleaming en-suite bathroom. Her body was impressive. Tall. Lean. Not an inch of fat. But there were curves, accentuated by her firm and full breasts.

She stared impassively into a spotlessly clean mirror. Her youthful features were still apparent – just – on a world-weary and prematurely aged face. She ran her strong trigger finger down the ragged vertical scar lining her right cheek. It was still there. A furrow of red marking her out from the pack. As indelible as a Tahitian warrior's tattoo.

Charly stepped into the power shower, tilted her head forward and pressed the button. The water battered her taut shoulders and washed away the remnants of another troubled night's sleep.

Immaculately dressed in a black business suit, Charly munched her high-fibre cereal and studied a mute TV. A News programme was broadcasting images of a burning oil rig in the middle of an angry sea. The breaking news ticker taped along the bottom of the screen – "Oil pollution threat grows in the Arabian Sea as a Carrington Trust Petroleum rig continues to burn out of control."

Charly grabbed the remote and killed the post-apocalyptic scenes. She jumped to her feet and headed for the hallway. Patent leather briefcase in hand, she punched in an alarm code and exited her luxurious but soulless one-bedroomed apartment.

A scruffy but cheerful street seller hawked his 'Homeless' magazines on the pavement outside an enormous Canary Wharf glass monolith. Above the entrance to the apparently recession-proof building, bold black letters proclaimed to the world that this was the global headquarters of Carrington Trust Petroleum.

Charly brushed aside the upbeat vendor and headed for the opulent edifice. The hawker just shrugged his shoulders. He was used to being treated like shit by 'the suits', and Charly was, most definitely, 'a suit'.

As Charly passed the bull-necked security guard protecting the magnificent revolving door, a bee buzzed past her head. She instinctively lashed out with her briefcase and squashed the insect against a wall. No prisoners. Some things never change.

Like Jonah being swallowed by the whale, Charly disappeared into the building.

Charly marched out of a glass elevator and into the open-plan office of the tenth floor. It was like entering a giant hive. Sharp-suited workers prattled into phones, stared into VDUs and buzzed about conducting impromptu meetings on the hoof.

Stone-faced, Charly strode across the vibrant floor in silence. No greetings or acknowledgements. She was the eye of the tornado.

A chirpy male worker looked up at her as she passed. 'Morning, Miss Stevens,' he said playfully.

Charly ignored the runt and marched up to a door displaying a shiny brass nameplate – "Charlotte Stevens, Development & Logistics Manager, Arabian Division." She entered the office and slammed the door shut. A portcullis would have been preferable to Charly, but a hefty wooden door had been the architect's preference so that would have to do.

The male worker smirked across at a bubbly female temp. She seemed curious and felt compelled to speak. 'What's wrong with her?' she asked.

'Army dyke,' he replied.

The temp looked surprised. 'She was in the army?'

'O-F-F-I-C-E-R. Bit of a female Rambo. Got the Military Cross for topping Terry Taliban,' said the male worker as he winked. 'But I'd watch out if I were you. It's not my weapon she wants to inspect.'

The temp appeared taken aback. 'You mean she's a...'

'What do you think? Makes Hannibal Lecter look like a bereavement counsellor.'

Charly was perched behind a large mahogany desk. She appeared to be sitting to attention. If her hand had suddenly sprung up and saluted, it wouldn't have looked out of place.

Scowling as usual, she ripped a phone off its hook and hammered in three numbers. 'There's a vagrant causing a nuisance outside the building,' she shouted into the phone. 'Move him on. If he doesn't, call the police.' She slammed the phone down.

So it was official. Despite all her multifarious and impressive achievements, Charly had yet to find time to enrol in 'Charm School'.

She sat motionless for a while. It was as if her brain was rebooting. Her eyes became fixed on a large photograph on her desk. A man of about forty, wearing a British Army officer's uniform, stared back from the picture. A description at the bottom of the frame revealed the identity of the soldier – "Major Dan Stevens, VC, 1940-1982".

A knock on the door. Charly's staring eyes blinked as she returned from her reverie. 'Enter,' she barked.

An ineffectual male probationer meekly opened the door.

Instead of greeting her visitor, Charly targeted her gaze downwards towards a file on her desk. 'Sit,' she said without looking up.

The probationer shuffled towards the chair in front of Charly's desk. Given the body language on display it was a miracle he reached the seat. In fact, it was miraculous that he could move at all. Dead man walking, as they say.

The dispirited man flopped down into the seat with a bowed head. It looked as if he had consumed a bowl of tranquillisers for breakfast.

Charly finally raised her head and glared at her sacrificial victim. Nothing like a nice bit of face-to-face empathy to enhance staff morale. She opened up with her first salvo. 'You knew what was expected of you during the probationary period?'

Of course he knew. That's why he appeared totally fucked. The man nodded and forced a strained smile.

'You haven't delivered,' she continued.

The probationer's head rose slightly and he grimaced; as if he was strapped to a medieval rack and his torturer had clicked it up a notch.

Time for the fight back.

'There's been...I've had a lot of...ehm...personal things happen recently. Kind of bad timing,' he related in a monotone voice filled with resignation.

Charly stared at the man in silence. Was that it? she thought. Was that the sum total of your defence?

The man squirmed in his seat as he played the only card left in his sorry pack. 'My wife and I have just had our first baby. Medical complications,' he explained.

Checkmate. Surely? No one with a properly functioning cardiac system could ignore this desperate plea. Charly just looked back down at the file and muttered the inevitable. 'Human Resources will take you through the Exit process. That's all.'

***

A fifty-year old man strolled along Hyde Park inhaling the varied scents of the summer blooms. His name was Frederick Archer – a Machiavellian MI6 Controller conservatively dressed as a 'City Gent'. With each confident stride he nonchalantly twirled his black rolled-up umbrella.

The muffled ringtone strains of "Land of Hope and Glory" struggled to be heard beneath Archer's black Crombie overcoat. He stopped, slid his hand into the inside pocket and pulled out a very Smart phone. He placed the mobile to his ear.

'Yes,' he said into the phone. 'I see. Of course it must.' After a pause, he continued. 'No time to lose, then. Do let the cowboys know that we will initiate as soon as possible. And I will arrange the…ehm…insurance policy.'

Archer smirked. He liked listening to the sound of his own refined voice. He spoke again into the phone. 'Absolutely. Can never be too careful.' A final pregnant pause. 'Oh, I will. You can be sure of that. Goodbye.'

As Archer returned the phone to his coat pocket, a female jogger ran past. He caught her eye and smiled, with a slight bow of his head. The charmed jogger smiled back. 'Delightful,' he muttered to himself. Archer liked to bestow gifts and was therefore please by her gratified response.

He meticulously smoothed down his overcoat, swung his umbrella up to his shoulder and marched off whistling.

***

Classical portraiture adorned the walls of a large and opulent office. A tall figure stood gazing out of an expansive window at the modern office blocks littering London's Docklands. His name was William Milhouse, a distinguished, middle-aged 'Oxbridge Establishment' man.

A firm knock on the door drew his attention away from the sprawling vista. 'Come,' he said in a baritone voice.

Charly entered. A beaming Milhouse pirouetted round.

'Charlotte, please have a seat,' he said as he beckoned his visitor over to a suite of leather armchairs beside the full-length window.

Charly padded across the plush carpet and sat down. Milhouse joined her.

He poured a cup of coffee from a steaming jug. 'I take it you've seen the media images?' he asked, handing the cup to Charly. She nodded. He continued. 'Dante's Inferno. We're now flavour of the month with Greenpeace, the Yemen Government has jumped onto the environmental bandwagon and the global press can sense blood as our shares plummet into the abyss.' He picked up a plate of biscuits. 'Care for one?'

'No thank you,' replied Charly.

Milhouse threw her an approving look. 'Quite right. Bad for the waistline. I can see that you look after yourself. Appearances count, don't you think?'

No reaction from Charly. She didn't think about appearances so whether they counted or not was irrelevant. That's why she appeared to most people as an unfeeling bitch.

Milhouse could tell he was mining an unproductive seam. He cleared his throat and cut to the chase. 'We need to ensure a radical PR initiative is implemented in full view of the World Press. The moral high ground must be regained.'

Charly looked bemused. What the fuck had morality got to do with plundering oil from the Middle East? Further clarification was required. 'A PR initiative?' she asked.

Milhouse was more than happy to articulate the position. 'Some kind of humanitarian relief programme in their back yard. God knows, the people there need one.' He paused and leaned forward for effect. 'I'd like you to organize this. Speak to your brother. We'd offer his agency unlimited finance, within reason of course.'

This flustered Charly. It seemed like she'd been bushwhacked and she certainly knew what that felt like. Her uncertainty was obvious as she stuttered out her response. 'I'm not sure Ben would be able to arrange something like this at such short notice.'

Milhouse was having none of it. This wasn't a request. She surely knew that? 'Oh, I'm sure he'd listen to his big sister,' he proclaimed. 'Especially when Third World lives could be saved.' He went for the jugular. 'Presumably your brother has taken the Hippocratic oath?'

Charly sat stony-faced, unimpressed with her boss's bullshit. You're one sneaky fucker, she thought.

Milhouse smiled in a vain effort to thaw her out. Time for the coup de grâce, he calculated. 'And…err…our only condition is that you accompany him and his people to Yemen.'

What the fuck? Charly could not get her head around this crap. 'Why me?' she asked, with more than a hint of desperation.

'You're a woman and you're fluent in Arabic. As the representative of Carrington Trust Petroleum I want you to exercise your feminine wiles. Dress like a nun, cry like an Oscar winner and hug a few malnourished babies. I'm sure the press will do the rest.'

Charly was panicking and blurted out the only thing she could think of. 'I'm not really good with children.'

This was the understatement of the century but it was nowhere near sufficient to derail Milhouse. He smirked as he clinched the deal. 'I'm sure your maternal instincts will come to the fore when required.'

A shell shocked Charly could only frown. She'd run out of road. For a few seconds there was a very uncomfortable silence.

'Well,' Milhouse finally said, 'that's settled.' He grinned like a Rollover lottery winner. 'More coffee? It's Mocha.'

CHAPTER 3

East End of London. The scabby part. Polar opposite to the shining glass behemoths of Canary Wharf.

Charly marched down a bedraggled street which epitomized the global downturn. A line of charity shops and boarded-up windows were punctuated at the end by a shabby office, identified above its uninviting entrance as the base for 'Med Team International Relief'. Obviously, the 'relief' had yet to extend to the organization's premises.

Charly entered the office.

The interior suggested more 'anarchist collective' than 'medical aid agency'. Global health initiative posters festooned the flaking walls. Large plastic bags and boxes cluttered the floor space. It was a dump.

Annie, the heavily pierced office gofer, stood checking a consignment of rehydration kits. Her dreadlocks sailed round as she glanced up and spotted Charly. 'Hi Charly. Ben's in the back,' she said with a broad smile.

Charly nodded but didn't crack a smile herself. Which was probably just as well, because if she had then Annie would have had assumed that she was on medication or experiencing some form of executive breakdown. Annie had never classified Charly as the 'smiling' type.

Charly picked her way through the boxes and bags to the rear of the office. Annie just shrugged and resumed her checking.

The back room was a glorified cupboard. Ben Stevens, a youthful and relaxed thirty-year old doctor, sat peering at a computer screen busy with an array of numbers which seemed to favour the debit column of an Excel spreadsheet. Perhaps he thought that if he stared hard enough and long enough at the screen then the numbers would magically transform and start to add up. However, his concerned look and shaking head suggested otherwise.

'Hi Ben,' said Charly.

Ben turned and a beaming smile filled his affable face as he saw his adoptive sister. In life's lottery, he had acquired a 'happy gene' and was very obviously yin to Charly's yang.

'Hi Sis. Thought our date was tomorrow night?' he said.

'Correct,' replied Charly, 'but something's cropped up and I need to talk to you now.'

'Lost your mobile?'

'Official business.'

This got Ben intrigued. 'Official business? Well. Better take a seat.'

Ben stretched across and brushed away an empty pizza box balancing on a grotty chair. Charly looked at the stained seat as if it was occupied by a steaming pile of shit. 'Nice one,' she said sarcastically.

'Fancy a coffee?' offered Ben

'No. I'd rather get out of here in one piece.'

Ben grinned. 'Okay smart arse. Fire away.'

Charly began her pitch. 'Carrington Trust Petroleum…'

Ben interrupted. 'I knew it! I just knew it!'

Charly paused and glowered at Ben. With a teasing grin, he gestured with his hand for her to continue. 'Carry on. I'm sitting comfortably,' he chuckled.

An irritated Charly tried again. 'Carrington Trust Petroleum is prepared to finance you to take a medical relief team to the Yemen.' She stopped. An awkward silence.

This wasn't what Ben expected but he thought he'd better say something so he did. 'Are they indeed?'

Charly nodded. 'But you must leave with me in three weeks.'

Ben sat calculating his options. Probably a 'no brainer' given the parlous financial state of his agency but he still couldn't resist getting a dig in. 'I see,' he said. After a long pause, he continued. 'Would this act of medical charity have anything to do with a Carrington Trust Petroleum rig currently spewing out oil into the otherwise pristine Arabian Sea?'

Charly couldn't hide her growing irritation. 'Why are you so cynical?'

'I'm not cynical, Charly. I'm also not stupid.'

A petulant Charly sprang to her feet. 'Forget it! I knew this was a bad idea.' She turned to leave.

Ben jumped up. He glanced at the unhealthy fiscal data polluting his computer screen, did an instant calculation and shouted after Charly. 'Hang on, hang on. I didn't say I wouldn't do it.'

It was clear his sister's patience was about to snap. 'Ben, I don't have time to fuck about with this.'

'How much finance?' queried Ben.

'Unlimited. Within reason, of course.'

A big smile on Ben's face confirmed that the deal was clinched. 'Well, of course. Sit back down, young lady.' He shouted through to the front office. 'Annie!'

***

A loquacious DJ prattled in the background of a congested and noisy London pub. Charly and Ben were holding up the bar and hollering to each other over the thumping beat. Ben cupped his hand by his mouth to amplify a question. 'Tasmanian devil returned recently?'

'I would have told you,' said Charly, shaking her head.

'Because I'm a doctor?'

'Because you're my brother.'

Ben took a gulp of his pint before getting to the point. 'So taking the meds as prescribed?'

Charly half-smiled. 'I always do what I'm told.'

Ben choked with laughter and spat out a mouthful of lager. Charly gave her brother a disapproving shake of the head then grinned. 'How's Boo-Boo?...or Choo-Choo?...or...'

'Lulu?' Ben suggested.

'That's the very chap,' said Charly, nodding her head. 'How could a girl called Lulu be allowed to study medicine?'

Ben couldn't let that one pass. 'Yeah, I know. About as ridiculous as a girl called Charly being allowed to wield a heavy-duty machine gun.'

Charly raised her pint in a drunken toast. 'With lethal intent.'

Ben reciprocated with his glass. 'With lethal intent. Cheers!'

Both their heads tilted back as they quaffed their pints.

'Are you still shagging her?' asked Charly.

'Unfortunately not. Ex-boyfriend reappeared.'

'One of those, was she? Why are women so needy?'

Ben realized that Charly was actually being serious. 'They're not,' he replied. ' It's just that some of them have feelings.'

'Christ!' uttered a disgusted Charly.

A drunk male staggered up to the bar and wrapped his arm around Charly's slim waist. 'How ya doing, gorgeous?' he slurred.

Charly glowered at the interloper. 'Remove your fucking arm before I snap it in two.'

Ben intervened. 'Easy Charly.'

But the drunk man persisted. 'Yeah. Keep your tits on. Just having some fun.'

Ben tried to appeal to the man's better nature. 'Maybe if you look for it somewhere else? We're a bit busy here.'

The inebriated pest giggled at Charly. 'You're not with that twat, are you?'

Ben eyeballed his sister. 'Let's go. Now!'

Charly squared up to the drunk, grinned then turned away and headed for the exit with her brother.

'Slag!' the man shouted after her.

That stopped Charly in her tracks. Ben knew what was coming next so he grabbed his sister's arm. 'Don't,' he said firmly.

Charly wrenched her arm free and sauntered back to the smirking drunk. She stared. He blinked first. 'You just couldn't resist it, could you?' she said coolly.

'And what the fuck are you going to do about it?' he spat back.

Whack! Charly's fist smashed into the drunk's face. There was a cracking of cartilage and bone as the man collapsed to the floor cupping his shattered nose. An impassive Charly massaged her bloody knuckle as shocked customers looked on.

Ben dragged his sister away. The two siblings bustled through the ogling throng as two burly bouncers followed in keen pursuit.

Ben and Charly stumbled out the pub and raced up the street. The two bouncers stopped outside the door. They had reached the border of their jurisdiction and could only gnash their gums as they watched their targets flee.

After a minute, Ben and Charly stuttered to a halt outside an Underground station. Ben was doubled-up and breathless. Charly grinned at her out of shape brother. 'Now that was fun.'

Ben just shook his head. 'You are a sociopath.'

An unusually playful Charly protested. 'Come on. You enjoyed that. Admit it.'

Ben broke into a reluctant smile. 'Nobody would believe that we were related.'

'We're not,' Charly blurted out.

Both of them instantly knew that she hadn't meant to say that. There was an uncomfortable silence as high spirits rapidly deflated.

Ben realized that he had to save the situation. Didn't he always? So he placed a brotherly arm around his sister. 'Time for a kebab, my dear,' he suggested.

'Doner,' she specified.

'OK, Shish,' Ben said in his best Sean Connery accent.

Charly burst out laughing. 'Did you mean to say that, Mr Bond?'

Ben gurned at his sister.

'Just for that,' she said, 'you're paying.'

CHAPTER 4

A meticulously manicured lawn, surrounded by well-tended flower beds and hedges, lay at the back of a Georgian terraced house. This was London property at its most affluent and desirable.

Gloved and formally casual, William Milhouse pruned some flower stems with his gardening shears. This was his oasis of calm.

Bees flitted about gathering their nectar. Milhouse's gaze followed the industrious insects as they buzzed through the balmy air. His calm face filled with a luxuriant smile as he pondered the apian wonders of the Universe.

Milhouse was used to obeying orders. Chain of command and all that. Although sometimes he wondered where, and if, the buck actually stopped. These orders were man-made, he had decided, and therefore the product of an inherently flawed system. On the other hand, the artifice of instruction was redundant for bees. They did what they had to do instinctively and perfectly, behaviour crafted by millions of years of Darwinian evolution. Nature at its glorious best, and certainly not the result of some fucking prick ordaining it to be so. No. Didn't those people up the chain, those wankers, realize that they were constantly out of their depth? As Doris Day so succinctly put it, "que sera, sera". You could swim all you wanted but that tide – that merciless, unforgiving, unrelenting tide – would always wash you back to the rocky shoreline. Two hundred thousand years, at best, of thrashing about in oceans and stumbling around rocks, deserts and forests. And the sum total of that? We'd built up an impressive portfolio of the most persuasive reasons and efficient methods for killing each other. The bees would always have the edge, Milhouse concluded. There could be no argument or discussion about that. It was as certain as rain on an English summer day. And, let's face it, that was as certain as it could fucking get.

A female voice floated out from the back door. It was Milhouse's prim and proper fifty-something wife, Bridget. 'Fancy a G and T?'

Milhouse turned and nodded at his smiling spouse.

'Coming right up, darling,' she said as she disappeared into the house.

Milhouse drew a tired-looking branch towards him and snipped it with the shears. The excised wood dropped to the emerald-green lawn.

*****

Charly was back in the East End. She walked up to a non-descript building, hesitated for a few seconds, then entered.

Ronald Stone, a pugnacious middle-aged cockney, sat behind his tidy desk. Charly sat facing him.

Stone was ex-military and now working as a Private Investigator. He'd been round the block a few times and could usually size people up in a matter of seconds. But Charly was a challenge. It wasn't so much that she exuded mixed signals, it was just that she seemed to transmit nothing. Just a deafening radio silence.

Stone's first question to his inscrutable client was a simple one. 'Do you know which hospital it was?'

And Charly had a simple answer. 'No. But it was apparently in the Manchester area.'

'Apparently?' Stone asked.

'I don't know for sure. That's why I'm paying you.'

'I can certainly find the required information,' he said. ' What you do with it is up to you.' Talking about stating the blindingly obvious, Charly thought, but she nodded anyway. Stone continued. 'In my experience, not every adoptee wants to contact their birth parent once they've been located. Maybe worth thinking about.'

'I have. That's why I'm here.'

'Sure?'

'I'm sure.'

That was the green light Stone required. 'Okay, once we get the paperwork and finance processed, I'll start the search.'

'Timescale?' asked Charly.

'Days rather than weeks. I'll be in touch.'

Charly stood up. 'Thank you.'

***

Charly entered the hallway of her flat and lobbed a set of keys onto a small wooden table. The keys landed with a clatter beside an antiquated answering machine. She checked the machine – "No messages."

She kicked off her shoes and wearily shuffled into the kitchen. Filling a glass of water from that tap that never seemed to work properly, she downed another two capsules. She wrenched open her unfeasibly large but sparsely stocked fridge and grabbed a solitary lump of mouldy cheese. She sniffed the offending item and grimaced. Mature was one thing, but rancid? The cheese was binned.

Charly poured herself a super-sized glass of red wine. As she lifted it for that first morale-boosting infusion, the hallway phone rang. Fuck it! She ignored the caller and gulped the wine back. It was all about priorities.

After another large draft of the vine, Charly padded into the hallway and played the recorded message on her answering machine. 'Hi! It's Ben. Make sure you arrange an appointment tomorrow for all your inoculations. We leave in only two weeks. And remember to pack your AEDs. Love you.'

A smile infiltrated Charly's hard face. There weren't many things in life which could initiate such a response from her but the sound of Ben's voice was most certainly one.

Charly carried her bountiful glass of wine into the living-room. Slumping into a spongy leather two-seater settee, she grabbed her laptop from a coffee-table and flicked the screen open. Within seconds, she was staring intently at an email message opened up in her In-Box. The communication was clear and to the point – "Dear Miss Stevens, I have located your birth mother. Her contact details are: Muriel Young, 15 Highgrove Terrace, Manchester M47. Tel 0161 552 7761. Kind regards, Ronald Stone."

Charly kept staring at the details on her screen. Reading and re-reading. Finally, her trembling hand picked up a mobile phone. Ready to dial. She glanced at the laptop screen and punched in the first four numbers. She hesitated before inputting another three numbers. A further pause. Her eyes clenched shut and her face creased with stress. That Rubicon had to be crossed. She knew it. Of course she fucking knew it. Christ, even Ben had done it. No problems there. Quite the opposite. It seemed to have gone well. So what was the problem? What was HER problem?

Charly hurled the phone onto the floor, slammed shut the laptop screen and drained her glass of wine. It would have to wait. Maybe when hell froze over as a pig flashed across the scarlet hued sky?

***

It was one of those busy London wine bars - a different exotic theme every night and infested by rabid 'young professionals'. It smelled of easy money and the constant hubbub gave a new meaning to that hoary old phrase, "the chattering classes."

A nervous Charly sat waiting alone in a corner. Her hand was anchored to a double gin and tonic and she looked as if she would rather be at the Dentist waiting for a double wisdom tooth extraction without anaesthetic. She checked her watch then glared up at the large 'retro' clock above the bar. Christ! Who designed this fucking place? she mused.

Seconds later, her blind date breezed in. Tall, handsome, mid-thirties. He scanned the bar area and finally spotted Charly simmering in her seat. She was the only person in the establishment sitting alone so it was a safe bet that he'd found his squeeze for the night. He sauntered up to her.

'Are you Charly?' he asked. A curt nod of the head confirmed his assumption was correct. 'I'm Robert,' he said triumphantly. It was evident that this was a fact of which he was particularly proud.

Charly looked as if she wanted to tear his smug face off then kick him in his cosmetically-waxed balls. 'Our appointment was for eight,' she barked.

Robert smiled his charming smile and tried to placate his new pissed-off friend. 'You mean our date?' he clarified. 'It's only ten past. I'm sorry. Rush hour traffic.' His rational defence should have assuaged the ire of most normal human beings but, unfortunately, Charly didn't quite fit into that category.

'You should have considered that possibility and left earlier,' she thundered in reply.

Robert shook his head in disbelief. He wasn't used to women speaking to him in that tone. That was not how it worked. In fact, for him it was debateable as to whether women should be allowed to speak at all. Time to redesign his evening. 'You know what?' he said to Charly, 'I've just realized I'm running late for another appointment.' And with that, Robert petulantly stormed out of the bar.

The gaze of nosy customers followed Robert's exodus then shifted to Charly - perhaps in the expectation of some tears, carpet-chewing or at least a bit of hand-wringing from the rejected spinster in the corner. But a defiant Charly just glowered back at them. Intimidated eyes were quickly averted.

Half an hour later, Charly entered the award-winning French restaurant she had booked up weeks before. She strode up to the Maitre d' and updated him on the revised dining requirements. 'Table booked for Stevens. Just for one. The other party couldn't make it.'

As Edith Piaf warbled in the background, the exceedingly bald head waiter led Charly into an intimate dining area populated by romantic couples. He withdrew the seat from a candlelit table. She gave him an awkward smile as she sat. He fashioned a dignified retreat.

Charly cleared her throat then pulled out a folded copy of the FT from her bag and began to read.

CHAPTER 5

The Yemen valley plain was stiflingly hot, unlike the mountain cave the leper had left two hours before.

He stood for a moment filling his lungs with the arid air. Positioned in front of him were his ten long, thin bee hive boxes. These were hollowed-out logs which lay flat on a large wooden trestle. Although stacked and roped together with twine, they appeared as if they had naturally sprouted from the desert floor.

The leper was fully robed and fully armed. A tightly wound dark cotton fabric covered his face like a Tuareg headdress. Only his haunted black eyes remained visible.

His robes fluttered in the light wind as he hobbled up to his hives. V-shaped pieces of wood covered the entrance to each hollow log. A procession of bees buzzed in and out of the front of each log.

The leper shuffled to the back of one hive. He rammed his clawed hand through a baked mud seal and pulled out a fresh honeycomb. He deposited it into a sack and repeated the process. The harvesting of the honey continued for another fifteen minutes until the sack was full.

With the bulging sack draped over one shoulder, and his AK47 slung over the other, the leper limped along a dusty path. The faraway roar of engines broke the peaceful silence. The alert leper's head swivelled round. He shielded his eyes with a hideously twisted hand and peered into the distance. Clearly panicked, he hurriedly jerked towards the tree line. The heavy sack slid off his shoulder and fell into the dust. He hesitated. The honey needed to be retrieved but that roar got louder. There was no time. He abandoned the sack, took cover behind a line of trees and readied his weapon.

Two Land Cruisers rumbled towards the leper's position. He took aim from behind a tree. The thundering machines flashed past in a swirl of sand. Then there was a shout. The vehicles braked sharply, reversed and slewed to a halt beside the discarded sack.

Armed men in Arabic dress filled the back of both Cruisers. The concealed leper kept his AK47 trained on the men as they sat and chatted in the open wagons.

The bearded driver of the first vehicle stepped out. The man was in his thirties and wore a black eye-patch, but he was still recognizable as the battle-scarred Taliban commander who had attacked Charly's Land Rover in Afghanistan five years before.

Vigilant and suspicious, Khalid slowly scanned the area with his one good eye. He looked down and saw the discarded sack of honey and smiled. He picked it up and dug his hand inside, pulling out a lump of honey and stuffing it into his mouth.

The leper had Khalid in his gun sight. His gnarled finger quivered over the trigger.

Khalid smirked as he greedily devoured the honey. His men watched in respectful silence as he licked his sticky fingers clean then returned to his vehicle. He threw the honey sack into the cabin and jumped back into the driver's seat.

The two vehicles accelerated away. The leper lowered his weapon as his unblinking eyes watched the unwelcome visitors disappear into a heat haze.

***

Shiny contraptions, designed to exercise every conceivable muscle of the human body, stood arrayed along the gleaming floor like metallic soldiers on parade.

The scent of fresh sweat hung in the air as perspiring bankers, dentists and estate agents jogged, cycled and rowed to the pounding beat of four-to-the-floor House music.

Charly was in her state-of-the-art London Gym. She lay on her back with a contorted expression on her face. Her taut body strained with every muscle and sinew and her strong arms quivered with an almost superhuman effort. She forced out a muffled guttural scream as she bench-pressed a ridiculously large weight.

Muscled male weightlifters gawped in admiration at the apparently testosterone-fuelled Amazon within their midst.

Charly rested for a moment and stared up at the white antiseptic ceiling of the weight room. There was a steely determination in her eyes. But also something more. Something sad. An aching emptiness.

***

Aden's seafront promenade was scalding to the touch. If someone had desired an impromptu omelette then a dozen eggs and the sandy pavement would have been sufficient for the task.

An Arabic man in his thirties pushed his aged father in a wheelchair. His eight-year old son skipped along, smiling broadly and holding his seated grandfather's limp hand.

The man was Ahmed al-Hamali. A cheery and plump local dressed in a Keffiyeh headdress, crisp business suit and traditional wraparound skirt. The traditional curved dagger of Yemen rested against his swollen belly.

Ahmed's mobile phone rang. He stopped, pulled the phone out of his jacket and pressed it to his ear.

As Ahmed took the call, the boy tended to his senile grandfather.

Ahmed listened intently to the garbled English voice without interruption. His sunny demeanour quickly darkened as he ended the call. 'OK,' he said into the phone. Grim faced, he slid the mobile back into his jacket and resumed pushing the wheelchair.

Sensing the change in his father's mood, the boy's exuberant smile evaporated.

***

An early London morning in the seedier part of town. The ambience was 'back street' vice, neatly emphasized by the nervous flickering of a garish neon Hotel sign.

In one of the hotel's grotty rooms, water dripped from a cracked ceiling onto a torn mattress. 'One Star' accommodation was probably pushing it.

A naked man and woman lay stretched out on the damp bed. The female was still asleep but the man was stirring. He yawned and sat up. Muscled and lean, he possessed an impressive physique which seemed out of odds with the dilapidated surroundings.

The naked man was an MI6 Field Agent called Colin Smith. Aged forty and with a bushy beard, he looked like a Geography teacher taking a menopausal walk on the wild side. But. When he moved, he moved like a predatory beast.

Still unclothed, he stood up, stretched and prowled to the window. Like a man used to hiding in the shadows, he positioned himself sideways and stole a cautious look out. The back street was empty. He eased open the cracked window a few inches and lit up a cigarette. He ingested a lungful of tar and hacked out an early morning cough.

Ten minutes later, Smith was casually dressed. He prodded his sleeping partner and she snorted awake. He threw a crumpled fifty-pound note onto the bed. The female smiled but there was no flicker of emotion from her older client. Just dead eyes. Like a shark.

A silent Smith walked to the door and left. The female swept up the cash and resumed her slumber.

Feeding time and London Zoo was busy.

Frederick Archer stood in a crowd and watched the lions devour their breakfast. His trusty umbrella was hooked over one arm in anticipation of a downpour.

Colin Smith appeared by Archer's side as if he had just manifested out of thin air. There were no acknowledgements or greetings between the two spooks, just a furtive conversation as they gazed at the feeding beasts.

'Daniel. Now there's a name that would suit you,' said Archer.

Smith snorted with contempt. 'From an onomastic or religious allegorical perspective? Either way, it's bollocks.'

'Always a clever boy but don't overdo it,' said an unamused Archer.

'This should have been my day off,' protested Smith.

Archer laughed. 'And ever the joker. You do entertain me.' He stared at the lions. 'They look hungry.' He paused. 'Are you?'

'Where?' said an impatient Smith.

'Yemen.'

'When?'

'Tomorrow. Spot of babysitting,' clarified Archer.

'Just babysitting?'

Archer hesitated for a moment. 'Well…you know…maybe some subtle spoon-feeding as well. Be prepared. Boy scouts and all that.'

'Kit?' demanded Smith.

Archer smirked his annoying oleaginous smirk. 'My dear boy. In the kit shop. Where else?'

Smith melted back into the crowd. Archer glanced up at the threatening black sky, tutted and unfurled his umbrella.

***

The late morning downpour had been brief and the grass in St James's Park was hardly damp. That musty, almost consoling, scent of warm rain hung in the air.

William Milhouse strolled up to an empty bench and sat down. Ignoring the moist wood, he flicked open a broadsheet and started to read.

A minute later, Frederick Archer arrived. After meticulously wiping dry the wooden slats, he eased himself down on the other side of the bench. Neither man made eye contact or acknowledged the other's presence. They appeared strangers.

Archer hooked his umbrella over the arm of the seat, then delicately slid out a mobile phone from his coat. He placed the phone to his ear and started to speak softly. His words were for Milhouse and not the dead phone.

'Your man on the ground got everything under control?' he asked.

Milhouse put a deactivated phone up to his own ear. His smooth and confident air had evaporated and he was nervous. Archer was the boss and both men knew it.

'Yes,' Milhouse replied.

Archer didn't appear totally convinced. 'Good. Very good, ' he said. 'Make sure it stays that way. I'm sending one of my own boys out. Eyes and ears. Just in case. Apparently, he and your man are old University chums. Small world.'

Milhouse nodded his head reluctantly. It was bullshit, but what else could he do?

'They leave tomorrow?' asked Archer.

'Heathrow.'

'I want a clean innings,' said Archer. 'No dropped catches or run-outs. Keep it contained.'

Archer secreted the phone back into his overcoat, unhooked his brolly and slowly rose from the bench.

Milhouse remained seated.

Without saying another word, Archer sauntered away, swinging his umbrella like an RSM's pace stick and whistling a spot of Verdi.

CHAPTER 6

An isolated Yemeni village lay nestled within a barren sun-baked valley. Looming over the settlement was a spectacular mountain range, pressed up into the sky by a primordial and unstoppable force of ice and rock. The biblical colony seemed integrated with its savage surroundings. Rectangular mud brick houses were dotted around a whitewashed Mosque and every building appeared to have been born from the timeless lunar landscape.

Nasir, a carefree ten-year old goat herder, manoeuvred his bleating animals into a pen at the back of a five-storey tower house.

A guttural female voice screamed out. 'Nasir! Nasir!' It was a voice the boy dreaded. He quickly hid behind one of his goats and looked up.

Quismah, Nasir's intimidating and bad-tempered aunt, was peering down from the fifth floor of the house.

Nasir hugged the goat for reassurance and clamped his eyes shut in a vain effort to remain unseen.

Quismah quickly spotted her nephew and continued her bawling in Arabic. 'Come here now you little monkey! I can see you!'

Nasir remained still. Quismah drew on her extensive experience of child-rearing and hurled a clay pot down into the goat pen. She got through a lot of pots.

The missile smashed into the baked earth. Goats bleated in panic as clay shards peppered their pen. Nasir jumped up and raced out of the enclosure as if he was under shellfire.

Quismah screamed after him. 'Come back! Come back or I will beat you!'

But the boy just giggled as he ran away.

Nasir sat on the bank of a snaking mountain stream, allowing his tiny calloused feet to dangle in the chilled water. He smiled as he blew into a wooden flute.

Watching his reflection in the rippling water, he wafted his flute around in the air as he played. He was happy in this place.

Nasir's head tilted slightly as he caught the roar of Land Cruisers in the distance. He stopped playing and turned towards the rumbling engine noise. His smile evaporated and he scampered off.

Two Land Cruisers sped into the village. Apprehensive locals observed as the vehicles slid to a halt outside Nasir's house.

Bearded and turbaned men jumped from the back of the stationary Cruisers. Every man was armed with an AK47.

Khalid jumped out of the lead vehicle and marched into the house with his AK47 and the sack of honey. His men trooped in behind him.

In the open rooftop kitchen, Quismah stood at a table slicing raw meat. Her sturdy frame was fully robed but her jowly face remained uncovered and was fixed in a permanent scowl.

Khalid stormed in and dumped the sack of honey onto the table. 'Where is Jalilah?' he shouted in Arabic.

'I don't know,' Quismah replied.

Khalid jabbed his finger at the honey sack. 'This is for her.' Quismah threw her husband a contemptuous look. Khalid issued a warning. 'Only for her! If you or the boy touch it then I will beat you both.'

Quismah remained silent as she continued to dissect the meat.

Khalid stomped out. Quismah brushed the sack off the table. It crumpled to the floor and a honeycomb spilled out. She looked down and crushed it with her bare foot.

**

The Carrington Trust Petroleum conference room was full. A noisy battery of journalists, TV cameramen and photographers jostled for position in front of an elegant podium.

It was Showtime.

William Milhouse strode in from a side door and ascended the rostrum like a captain stepping onto the bridge of his ship. He spoke confidently into a glistening microphone. His plummy voice didn't crackle or falter; rather, it was clear and assured. The message was simple – "Crisis, what crisis?"

'Good morning, ladies and gentlemen. My name is William Milhouse and I am Director of Arabian Operations for Carrington Trust Petroleum. I realize that you may wish to ask questions relating to current remedial work being carried out in the Arabian Sea, however I would like to begin by announcing the following.'

Milhouse blinked as flash photography erupted throughout the room. Uninvited questions assailed the platform. Milhouse stared at the assembled media in silence. The hubbub died down.

'Thank you,' he said. After a pause, he continued. 'Carrington Trust Petroleum has funded in full a medical aid relief programme in Yemen. The team has already left the UK to start their life-saving work in the rural Hadhramaut region of the country. Dr Ben Stevens will lead the team which will focus on ante-natal care and screening for malnutrition in children.'

An agitated female journalist shouted out a question. 'Is this a desperate PR stunt to deflect attention away from your company's disastrous oil spill which is currently polluting the Arabian Sea?'

But this wasn't on the agenda. Milhouse cooly despatched his evasive reply. 'The President of Yemen has welcomed, and is grateful for, our medical assistance at a time of great need in his country.'

There was a hint of a smile on Milhouse's otherwise impassive face. He was in control. And he liked that.

***

Frederick Archer breezed up to the heavily guarded entrance of a UK Special Forces barracks. The military compound was surrounded by verdant English countryside. Archer looked around and inhaled the aroma of freshly harvested barley. The cultivation of both crops and war – how quaint, he thought, as he flashed his ID to an armed sentry and sauntered in.

Captain Anderson sat in the briefing room. Small, early thirties and dressed in 'civvies' he looked anything but an elite killing machine. He impatiently glanced at his watch and fidgeted like a sprinter waiting for the crack of the Starter's gun.

Without knocking on the door, Archer swept into the room and immediately expressed his insincere apologies for his tardiness. 'Sorry, old boy. I was promised a chopper but…cutbacks. You know how it is?'

The Captain glowered at Archer. He was a soldier and he hated 'suits', particularly ones filled with bullshit, and it showed.

Archer sat down, turned to the soldier and smiled. 'So here I am,' he trilled.

The Captain's icy demeanour remained frozen solid. It was evident that any charm offensive initiated by the visitor would fail.

An unperturbed Archer ploughed on regardless. 'Shall I begin?' There was a curt nod of the head from the intolerant officer. 'We have reports of an imminent threat to British nationals in the Yemen,' Archer said.

The Captain shook his head and a wry grin spread across his granite face. 'An imminent threat? In the Yemen? That's like saying it'll probably rain here in the next couple of days.'

'Splendid. Splendid. I like that,' said Archer as he forced a chuckle.

But there was nothing about Archer that the Captain liked. He just stared contemptuously at the Whitehall spook.

Archer got down to business. 'However,' he said, 'chatter from the bad boys seems to be transforming this from a forecast into a pretty damned good bet. You a gambling man, Captain Anderson?'

No answer from the taciturn soldier.

Archer continued. 'Thought not. I suspect that you like to deal in certainties. Control the odds, so to speak.'

The Captain stared at Archer in silence for a few moments. He was clearly sizing him up. Archer may have been a 'suit' but he was very well connected; that much the soldier could deduce. 'You're not Foreign Office, are you?' he stated.

'Career civil servant. Not a man of action like you,' said Archer, giving nothing away.

The Captain nodded. He now knew in his gut that Archer had been a fellow soldier. You could always tell. Eventually. Northern Ireland, perhaps? Or maybe 'Desert Storm'? Christ, it could even have been the Falklands. The man had killed. No doubt about that. And as far as the reference to a chopper was concerned, he was sure that a helicopter would not have been Archer's preferred choice of transport. Archer was 'old school' and the Captain imagined him as a Cavalry officer. The Light Brigade would have been more his style. A horseman. Yes, that was it. A horseman of the apocalypse. This biblical revelation clarified everything for the Captain. He now realized that whatever had brought Archer to this place, to his place, would soon involve the burning of villages and the letting of blood.

After a weighty silence, the Captain cut to the chase. 'When does my team need to be ready?'

'Three days. Usual base in Saudi. Further instructions to follow. Take your best men.'

'They are the only ones at my disposal.'

Archer smiled as he sprang from his seat. 'Indeed.' He glanced at his ridiculously expensive watch. 'Well. Mustn't keep you, Captain. Good luck.'

There was no 'au revoir' from the warrior. Just a stony silence.

Archer strode to the door, yanked it open and marched out.

As the door clicked shut, the Captain stared into space. He was thinking. Calculating. Working out the odds.

Captain Anderson's family lived in a modest detached house in greenbelt suburbia. A Nissan hatchback and a Vauxhall estate in the gravel driveway completed the domestic idyll. It didn't look like the refuge of an elite soldier, which was probably the point.

In his seven-year old daughter's bedroom, the Captain sat surrounded by posters of cute animals and a colourful collection of teddy bears. Hayley, his little girl, was cuddled up in her father's cosy lap. She clutched an extravagantly coiffured doll in her tiny hand.

'And they lived happily ever after,' he said, reading from a fairy-tale book.

'Was Beauty not scared of the Beast?' she asked.

'Of course she was.'

Hayley looked puzzled. 'So why did she go back to him? I think he looks scary.'

The Captain roared like a lion and tickled his daughter. She squirmed and giggled. 'Because she loved him,' he growled.

'Did she know he was a prince?'

'No. She loved him for what he was.'

Hayley screwed her face up in disgust. 'Yuck! Even though he was a beast?'

The Captain smiled. 'Yeah. Even though he was a beast.' He stood and carried his daughter to her bed. 'Cuddle up, now,' he said, tucking her in.

Hayley gazed up at her father. 'Are you going away again, daddy?'

'Just for a few weeks. You look after mummy.' He kissed her. 'Okay?'

Hayley smiled her sweet smile. 'Okay.'

The Captain walked into the living room. Vivienne, his pretty thirty-year old wife, was relined on a sofa reading a book. She looked up. 'Is she asleep?'

'Nearly,' he replied, easing himself down beside her.

He appeared tired and Vivienne was concerned. 'You alright?'

'Yeah. Fine,' he lied.

'You look worried, that's all,' she said, returning to her book.

The Captain picked up the TV remote and changed the subject. He was good at doing that. 'Let's watch a film,' he suggested.

'Saving Private Ryan?' she joked.

They both laughed, but only Vivienne was amused.

CHAPTER 7

The Yemen Republic Airways 747 was in flight. Ben and Charly sat together. She was in the window seat staring out at the infinite blue of a Middle Eastern sky.

Ben tapped his sister on the arm. 'Have you contacted her yet?'

'No.' Charly replied.

'Why not?'

She ignored the question and kept staring out of the window.

Ben persisted. 'Mum and Dad would have wanted you to do it.'

'Would they? We'll never know,' said Charly, still gazing out.

'I'm glad I did it,' said Ben. But Charly wouldn't take the bait and maintained an awkward silence. Ben continued. 'I know you and your company are using me. But I don't mind. For the greater good and all that.'

Charly finally turned towards her brother. 'At least one of us has a heart.'

Ben laughed. 'Cheer up Sis! One day your prince will come.'

Charly exploded. 'Fuck off, Ben. I'm not like you. I don't need anyone's approval.' She ripped the in-flight magazine from the seat pouch and buried her head in it.

Ben stared at his fuming sister. 'That's true,' he said sadly. 'You're not like me. You're not like anyone I know.'

Hidden by the magazine, Charly's moist eyes squeezed shut. Ben's words had hit home. He placed a reassuring hand on his sister's thigh. 'But I still love you,' he whispered.

Charly lowered the magazine, turned to her brother and reluctantly smiled. 'Smooth bastard,' she said.

The jet landed and taxied in the oppressive heat of Aden International Airport.

Ahmed al-Hamali stood waiting in the Arrival Hall holding up a sign – "Ben and Charlotte Stevens." Colin Smith strode out of the Customs area wearing a smart suit. The two men exchanged an almost imperceptible but knowing glance. The Arab's eyes followed Smith as he walked away. Unwelcome memories swirled around Ahmed's troubled mind.

It was nine years before, in a bustling Manchester University student canteen. A slimmer and younger Ahmed sat alone at a table. He pored over a text book as he wolfed down a large plate of rice.

A deliberately nondescript Colin Smith approached Ahmed's table. He was clean-shaven and dressed in the cheap, casual attire favoured by perennial mature students and MI6 campus recruiters.

'Mind if I sit?' he asked Ahmed.

Ahmed shrugged. Smith placed his lunch tray on the table. He unhooked his rucksack from his shoulder and placed it on the neighbouring seat. In Arabic tradition, Ahmed continued to shovel his rice down in silence.

Smith persisted. 'My name is Colin. Postgrad in Geology.' Ahmed ignored him and kept eating. 'You're Ahmed, aren't you? From Yemen.'

Ahmed stopped chewing. His dark eyes swivelled suspiciously towards his interrogator. He pushed his lunch tray to one side, snapped the book shut and gathered his coat.

Smith baited his hook. 'Your sister was a brave woman to defy the Taliban and teach in Afghanistan. She must have known that they would eventually kill her.'

Ahmed's curiosity overpowered his instinct to leave. 'Who are you?' he asked.

Smith smiled. 'I'm your friend. I share your beliefs. Radical Islamists are trying to destroy your country. First, the attack on the American warship in Aden harbour. Then New York...'

An Arabic student passed the table and greeted Ahmed. Smith was immediately silenced. He pretended to search for something in his rucksack, but it seemed as if he was trying to conceal his face.

The student left and Smith continued. 'The Americans know that many of the al-Qaeda leadership are from Yemen. They want revenge. And your neighbours in the Gulf do what the Americans desire. In fifteen years, Yemen's oil and water will run out. What then? Without friends, your country is heading for oblivion.'

'What do you want?' demanded Ahmed.

'The important question is what do YOU want,' countered Smith. 'You can help your country take a different path. In six months you will graduate with a First Class degree.'

Ahmed laughed. 'I'm an Arab, remember.'

'Precisely,' replied a stone-faced Smith. 'My friends will ensure that you are employed as site manager with a British oil company in Aden. We need somebody on the ground we can trust. A local who can blend in. Monitor the radicals. Keep us one step ahead.'

Ahmed stood. 'I think you have got the wrong man. You have made a mistake.'

'There's no mistake,' snapped Smith. Ahmed turned to walk away. Smith called after him. 'The militants know that your parents were strong supporters of the Marxist south before unification.' Ahmed froze. His face filled with dread. Smith continued. 'They don't like atheists. You are aware of what they will try to do. My friends can stop them.' Smith grabbed his rucksack and stood up. 'Think it over. Don't tell anyone about our chat. Your parents' lives are in danger. We need to keep them safe. I'll be in contact soon.' Smith walked away from the table and quickly melted into the background.

An airport tannoy boomed out. Ahmed blinked as if he had awoken from a hypnotic trance. The unbidden memories of his student days had finally receded and he was now back observing the multicultural throng of people that streamed out of the Customs area. Flowing robes, black veils and coloured turbans intermingled with western suits and jeans. The world was on display in front of Ahmed's watchful eyes.

Amidst the bustle, Charly and Ben emerged carrying backpacks. Charly spotted Ahmed's sign and pulled her brother towards their host.

Ahmed smiled at his visitors. Charly spoke first. 'Salam Alaikum. I'm Charlotte Stevens. You must be Ahmed. It's good to finally meet you in person.'

Ahmed briskly nodded at Charly then immediately turned to Ben and shook his hand. 'Wa-laikum as-Salam. I am Ahmed. Manager of the Aden office.'

Ben smiled. 'Hi. I'm Ben.' Ahmed's gaze remained locked on Ben. Charly knew he was avoiding eye contact with her. When it came to dealing with a woman in public, Arabic convention dictated clear rules of behaviour. Welcome to Yemen, she thought.

'You had a good journey?' Ahmed asked Ben.

'Yes, thanks.'

'I have booked you on a local bus to Hadhramaut,' said Ahmed. 'Incognito. Safer that way, Insha Allah.'

What little patience Charly possessed quickly ran out. 'Any armed guards?' she blurted out.

Ahmed replied, still looking at Ben. 'One. He is a good man. Discrete.' Ahmed formed the shape of a gun with his hand. 'And accurate.'

'Has the medical team arrived?' queried Ben.

Ahmed nodded. 'They will be waiting for you in the first village.'

'And the press?' asked Charly.

'All is arranged and will be well, Insha Allah,' replied Ahmed, still blanking Charly. 'Come. I will take you to the bus.'

***

A large bus bumped and rattled along an uneven strip of cracked asphalt. The potholed grey road snaked through a barren lunar landscape of desert, rock and scrubland. Craggy mountain plateaus loomed in the distance.

Local Yemenis filled the sweltering bus, many standing and swaying in the congested aisle. Charly and Ben sat together near the front in a growing pool of sweat. Their bodyguard sat behind them, his reptilian eyes constantly swivelling about as he checked for danger.

In the rear of the bus, four voluble Japanese tourists pointed out of the smeared windows and clicked their digital cameras.

The bus slowed. Charly craned her neck forward and squinted. A herd of goats was blocking the road. The bus slowly manoeuvred around the bleating livestock as they scattered in panic. An Arabic woman and a young boy stood at the roadside and watched as the bus crawled past. The woman was fully covered and veiled in black. Even the flesh of her hands was concealed by black gloves. An almost surreal-looking conical hat constructed of dried palm leaves sat atop her head. She looked like something Dorothy would have encountered on the Yellow Brick Road.

The young boy broke into a gap-toothed smile and waved at the bus. The enchanted Japanese tourists laughed and frantically waved back.

After another hour, the bus rumbled into a small settlement which consisted of a few single-storey mud houses and a handful of goats and donkeys. No women or children were in evidence but a group of men sat cross-legged in the shade of eucalyptus trees in the centre of the outpost. They gesticulated to each other as their bulging cheeks slowly masticated hallucinogenic Qat leaves.

The bus jolted to a stop in a cloud of dust. The local men ignored its arrival and continued to chew and chat.

Inside the bus, the rotund driver addressed his passengers in Arabic. 'We have stopped for fuel. Ten minutes.' He gestured with his hand to the main door. The passengers began to disembark.

A puzzled Ben looked at Charly. 'This isn't the right village. Why has he stopped?'

'Petrol,' she replied.

The ill-assorted passengers filed off and mingled by the side of the bus. The bodyguard hovered nervously beside Charly and Ben. The bus driver glanced furtively around then disappeared into one of the mud houses.

Charly checked her watch and dipped a hand into her jean pocket. 'Shit! I left my meds on the bus.'

There was a sound like a firecracker in the distance. The relaxed demeanour of the local Qat-chewing men immediately transformed into panic. They jumped to their feet and scattered into the surrounding houses.

The bodyguard immediately pushed Ben and Charly to the ground and ripped a high-powered handgun from his belt. 'Behind bus! Behind bus!' he screamed. In an instant, the minder's head exploded in a red mist and his legs buckled. The gun clattered onto the baked earth. Charly instinctively picked it up and dragged Ben to the other side of the bus.

The passengers screamed in terror as Khalid and his gang of armed terrorists emerged from behind the houses and charged towards them firing AK47s. The attackers bellowed out their war cry, 'Allahu Akbar! Allahu Akbar!'

Khalid sprayed a burst from his AK47 into the shocked Japanese tourists. Riddled with bullets, they crumpled to the ground in a blood-soaked heap.

'Get the English! Other side of the bus! Take them!' Khalid screamed to his men in Arabic.

Charly and Ben cowered behind the bus. Ben was clearly paralyzed with fear. Charly shook her brother. 'Ben! Run!' she hollered.

As the shooting and screaming continued, Charly and Ben sprinted past some mud houses and raced out of the settlement. Two of Khalid's men spotted them and took chase.

The two terrorists began to run down their prey, firing their AK47s on the move. Bullets zinged and swished past Charly and Ben as they hared past some trees and scrambled through a parched vineyard.

The terrorists were gaining fast. Ben slowed, stumbled then fell. Charly glanced back and saw her brother sprawled on the ground. She stopped and spun round. Gun in hand, she took careful aim. Crack! Crack! The bullets tore into the leading terrorist's chest and he fell dead into the dust. His companion dived behind a thorn bush for cover. Charly targeted the bush and fired another two rounds. The bullets seared over the head of the cowering man.

Charly hauled Ben up and dragged him away.

After a few moments, the terrorist peeked above the bush and saw Charly and Ben sprinting away into the desert landscape. He got to his feet, glanced down at his dead comrade and meekly headed back to the settlement.

Soaked with sweat and wheezing with exhaustion, Charly and Ben raced for their lives along the unstable desert terrain. Charly slowed and turned to her brother. 'Got your phone?'

Ben shook his weary head. 'On the bus.'

'Shit!' Charly said. 'Mine too.' Distant gunfire continued to crackle behind them. Charly glanced back. 'We've got to keep running.'

Back at the ambush site, petrified Yemeni survivors stood trembling with shock beside the bus. Some kneeled in manic prayer, hoping that Divine Intervention would somehow erase the savagery which was unfolding.

Khalid strutted around kicking the contorted bodies of his victims with his blood-soaked sandal. A Japanese man writhed in agony on the ground. Khalid shot him in the head. A badly wounded Japanese woman struggled to her knees. She clasped her quivering blood-spattered hands together and pleaded for her life. Khalid rammed the barrel of his AK47 into her face and fired. Brains, blood and bone splattered against the peeling paintwork of the bus. Khalid's men screamed with delight at the carnage. 'Allahu Akbar! Allahu Akbar!'

There was no more movement in the blood-drenched sand. The massacre was complete.

CHAPTER 8

After what seemed like an eternity, Charly and Ben staggered into a village at the foot of a mountainous volcanic range. There was little sign of life. Ben shuffled to a halt, crouched over and puked. A man on a donkey passed him in silence, glancing briefly at the vomit pooling around Ben's trainers. As usual, Charly was ignored.

'Are you alright?' Charly asked her brother.

Ben nodded as he wiped his chin clean. Charly's eyes slowly scanned the settlement. A few mud brick tower houses were scattered around a three-storey brick building which lay directly ahead; a dilapidated Arabic sign hung limply at an angle over its entrance. Charly nudged Ben and pointed at the building. 'Hotel. They should have a landline.' She stuffed the gun into her waistband and covered it with her sweat-stained T-shirt.

Charly and Ben entered the shabby hotel. A middle-aged hotel manager in a crisp white shirt and canary-yellow skirt emerged from a back room. A traditional curved dagger rested on his belly.

Ben slumped against the wall and slid wearily to the floor. Charly threw a tired smile at the man. 'God's peace be upon you,' she said in fluent Arabic.

'And God's peace be upon you,' he replied.

'We've been attacked by terrorists a few miles west of here. People have been killed and injured. We need to get help.'

'The phone lines are down and there is no mobile signal,' explained the manager. He grabbed a key and handed it to Charly. 'Go to this room on the third floor. I will see my neighbour. He can drive to the next police checkpoint and get help, God willing.'

'Thank you,' said a relieved Charly.

The manager nodded towards an AK47 lying on a table and smiled. 'You are safe here. You are my guests. I will protect you.' He pulled out two bottles of mineral water from a small fridge beside the reception desk and handed them to Charly and Ben. They greedily gulped down the chilled water.

Partially revived, Charly and Ben left the reception area and staggered up a steep flight of stone steps towards their room.

The manager waited a few moments, then picked up a vintage phone and dialled. The call was soon answered. 'God's peace be upon you,' the manager said into the phone. 'I think I have what you are looking for.'

There was no bed in the room. Just cushions scattered on the floor. Charly lay sleeping beside Ben, mumbling through a restless dream. She was back in Afghanistan. A grenade rocketed through the air and slammed into her Land Rover. An orange fireball roared into the sky.

Charly's eyes sprang open as she was roused from the dream. It was night and the room was now cloaked in darkness. A roar sounded outside the hotel window, like the engine of a truck turning over.

Charly scrambled to her feet and peered out the window. She could see armed terrorists, led by Khalid, spill out the back of two Land Cruisers. Khalid glanced up and caught Charly's face disappearing from view. He smiled and led his men into the hotel.

'Terrorists! Quick!' shouted Charly as she shook Ben awake.

Ben scrambled to his feet and they both dashed out the room.

In the hallway, they could hear Khalid's men shouting on the ground floor. Then there was the sound of footsteps running up the stairs.

Ben frantically looked about and spotted a window at the end of the hallway. 'Get that window open!' he shouted to his sister. Charly rushed to the window and struggled to open the jammed wooden shutters. She battered her fists against the wedged slats but they just wouldn't give.

Ben checked the stairs. A terrorist was charging up the steps. Ben grabbed a heavy wooden chest resting against the wall and hurled it down the stairs. The chest crashed into the terrorist and sent him tumbling backwards.

Ben sprinted to the window to help Charly. They both hammered desperately on the window in an effort to dislodge the stuck shutters.

Another terrorist reached the top of the stairs. His AK47 boomed in the hallway. Bullets slammed into the wall in a shower of plasterwork just above Charly's head. She spun round and ripped the gun from her waistband. Aiming at the terrorist, she squeezed the trigger. Click! The gun jammed. 'Shit!' screamed Charly as she hurled the gun at her attacker. It smashed into his head and he collapsed.

With one final savage effort, Ben managed to smash open the shutters.

'You first!' Charly screamed at her brother.

But Ben violently pushed his sister through the ragged window frame. 'I'm a doctor. You're ex-army,' he shouted.

Charly fell but managed to grab the external window ledge. She was hanging outside by her fingertips.

'Let go! It's your only chance!' Ben screamed. Charly looked up at her brother. He smiled. 'I love you,' he shouted.

A terrorist grabbed Ben from behind. As he fell back he managed to unhook Charly's fingers from the ledge.

'Ben!' screamed Charly as she plummeted to the ground. She landed with a squelch in a dung heap. Bullets cracked and ricocheted around her as the terrorists fired into the pitch blackness from the window above.

Charly scrambled to her feet and raced into the darkness. Bullets whizzed past her head as she ran, gasping, for her life.

Moments later, something heavy crashed into her back. It was as if someone had battered her shoulder blade with a lead mallet. She lurched forward and her left arm fell limply by her side. She could feel the warm blood as it trickled down the contour of her spine. Her body told her to stop but she resisted and somehow kept moving. 'Keep fucking going. Dig in!' she screamed to herself.

Charly battled through the night air. The bullets were no longer fizzing past her head but a primitive instinct compelled her to keep running. As she moved, she felt as if she was being sucked into a black hole and her fevered mind began to wander.

She was back in the Brecon Beacons. Just another sorry Sandhurst recruit struggling through the howling wind and sheeting rain. It seemed her feet were tramping on that desolate Welsh moorland and she remembered the oppressive weight of full bergen and regulation weapon which threatened to drive her into the sodden God-forsaken earth.

She saw herself slogging over the uneven terrain while a manic corporal ran beside her screaming encouragement into her frozen ear.

'You will keep going, Miss! Fucking harder!' he shouted.

Charly remembered that he had seemed small and frail but his voice boomed like a warrior so she had dug deep.

As her failing body slowed and tottered on the Yemen sand, that corporal's voice kept returning in her ear. 'They are chasing you because they want to kill you. Do you want to be fucking killed?'

Charly shook her weary head. Fuck you, she thought. But the voice was unrelenting. 'Do you want your men to be fucking killed?' he screamed. 'Do you?'

Charly gritted her teeth and howled. Her head shook in violent opposition to that annoying fucker's taunts. But the voice persisted. 'No! You do not,' he bawled. 'You will keep fucking running because your men need you alive. You will not give up. You will keep going, Miss! Won't you?'

Charly stumbled over a boulder but there was no mercy from that little shit. 'I said you will keep running,' the corporal railed.

A roar of defiance surged out of Charly's body and reverberated around the Yemen wilderness. Sand had transformed into rock and the mountain foothills were exacting their toll on a debilitated Charly. Her breathing had become laboured and she staggered again. She was fighting it but the effort was becoming too much.

Charly dropped to her knees, shivering and panting in the freezing night air. She mumbled to herself, 'Ben…' then collapsed unconscious onto the hard volcanic ground.

CHAPTER 9

A fiery orange ball rose in the Eastern sky. It was greeted by a plaintive melody which floated in the air and intermingled with the clanking bells and bleating of grazing goats.

Nasir skipped along a narrow path, herding his beloved animals as he played his wooden flute.

A screaming buzzard circled in the cloudless sky. Nasir halted, looked up and sniffed the air in an effort to detect the sweet scent of rotting flesh. He peered around the barren landscape and finally located the carcass. But it wasn't the body of an animal. He froze.

Nasir anxiously stared at the crumpled human form. The inanimate body moaned then jolted into life with the twitch of a bent arm. It was as if a bolt of lightning had surged through the cadaver. Nasir yelped and backed away. After a pause, he regained his courage and crept towards the reviving body.

The young goat herder stood over Charly and surveyed her blonde hair, pale face and female shape. Such a strange apparition, he thought. 'An angel,' Nasir muttered to himself in Arabic as his eyes filled with wonder. He threw his flute down and scampered away.

It was thirty minutes before Nasir returned with a donkey. He led the mangy beast up to Charly. She moaned again. He bent down and shook her. 'Angel, angel,' he said.

Charly's disorientated eyes flickered open and she mumbled through her parched mouth. 'Water.'

Nasir struggled to lift Charly. She grimaced with pain as the boy strained to raise her from the rocky ground. 'Don't angels have wings?' he complained to himself.

The boy gritted his teeth and helped Charly to inch herself up and hook a leg over the recalcitrant donkey. Unsteady on the saddle, she slumped forward over the donkey's mane as her mind was again consumed by blackness.

Nasir slapped the donkey's rump. It brayed in protest but reluctantly clip-clopped forward with Charly's leaden body swaying on top. The boy walked behind the ill-tempered beast of burden and clutched the back of his angel's blood-soaked shirt.

With one hand securing Charly's slumped body, Nasir led the sure-footed donkey into the mountain foothills.

After climbing a steep boulder-strewn slope, they eventually reached a plateau at the top of a rocky outcrop. This area was less barren and dotted with shrubs and small trees.

Nasir led the donkey through the trees and halted. He peered towards the partially concealed entrance of a small cave which looked as if it had been etched out of the volcanic rock. Outside the cave, a smouldering fire marked the centre of a rudimentary campsite. By the side of the cave entrance stood a primitive water well; basic but well-appointed, it consisted of a triangle of poles, attached pulley and leather bucket.

'Father! Father!' Nasir called out in Arabic.

The leper hobbled out of the cave. Shrouded in cloth from head to foot, only his piercing black eyes were visible. He bent down beside a neat pile of stones which rested by the mouth of the cave. He picked up a few pebbles and lobbed them, one by one, at Nasir.

'Go away,' the leper shouted in a hoarse voice. 'I told you, you are not welcome here. Leave!'

Nasir dodged the stones with practised agility. He pointed to Charly on the donkey. 'I have found an angel. Look.' The leper drew back his arm in readiness to strike again but hesitated. 'I think she has fallen and needs help. She is bleeding,' said Nasir.

'Take her off the donkey. Leave her on the ground and go.'

'But father, I can help you!'

'Do it!' the leper snapped back.

Nasir struggled hard but eventually pulled Charly off the donkey. Her limp body slowly slid onto the ground like a sack of corn. The leper watched in silence and made no movement. Nasir smiled at his father and waved, then turned around and led the donkey back down the slope.

The leper entered his cave and re-emerged with an AK47. He cautiously shuffled towards Charly's prostrate body. Probing her back with the gun muzzle, he located the entry wound of a bullet.

Charly stirred then groaned. The leper winced with pain as he bent onto one knee. His bandaged hand checked for an exit wound but there was none. The bullet was still lodged inside the angel.

The leper stood in front of the campfire with a beautifully ornate curved dagger strapped to the front of his waist. He bundled more kindling onto the fire until it was burning fiercely. He slowly unsheathed the dagger and thrust the blade into the heart of the flames.

Still unconscious, Charly lay next to the campfire. She was now on her front, face to one side.

A small bird flew out of a tree and perched itself on the leper's shoulder. He presented his twisted hand to the creature and it hopped onto his wrist as if it was a welcoming branch. 'Hello my little friend. I will feed you later. Now I have work to do,' said the leper, looking at the tiny bird.

The leper gently wafted his hand in the air and the bird flew off with a chirrup. He then crouched down, grasped the handle of the dagger and withdrew the red-hot blade from the fire

The leper knelt beside Charly and ripped away the back of her blood-caked T-shirt. He inserted the scorching blade into the entry wound and burrowed and twisted it inside her shoulder. Charly's flesh sizzled and she screamed. Seconds later, the bullet was flicked out.

A semi-conscious Charly writhed in agony on the ground. The leper pressed a poultice of Margosa leaves onto the raw wound then started to sing quietly in Arabic. Charly relaxed and began to snore. The leper's eyes smiled.

***

Hooded and trussed, the prisoner was bundled into a small, fetid room with an earthen floor. Only the flickering of candles illuminated the filthy interior. Closed wooden shutters sealed the makeshift cell from the outside world. Ben was literally boxed in.

A terrorist yanked the hood off and Ben's eyes squinted in the gloom. An AK47 dug into the small of his back and he was forced to his knees.

Khalid stormed into the room and loomed over his hostage. He pressed a handgun hard against Ben's temple. This was it, Ben was sure; his life would end right here, right now. 'Please, no!' Ben screamed in Arabic.

The empty gun just clicked. Ben quivered with terror. Khalid laughed and pistol-whipped his victim to the floor. Ben curled up in a foetal heap and started to moan. Khalid glared down. 'Soon, the British and American infidels will watch you die,' he shouted.

***

Nasir drove his goats through the village to the back of the tower house. He herded them into a small pen, ran to the rear of the house and disappeared inside.

The boy scampered up the steep stone steps and burst, breathless, into the open rooftop kitchen. Quismah was cooking rice on a stove. Her harsh and ugly face scowled at her nephew. 'Where have you been?' she asked in Arabic.

'One of my goats got lost, Aunt.'

Quismah slapped Nasir on the face. 'Don't lie to me!' she screamed.

Jalilah, a beautiful woman in her twenties, walked into the kitchen. Although dressed in black from head to foot, she was younger and more radiant than Quismah. 'Why are you beating your nephew again?' she asked Quismah. 'He's a good boy.' She smiled at Nasir. 'Aren't you?'

Nasir rubbed his battered cheek and glowered at the two women.

Jalilah tried to placate Quismah. 'Khalid will be home soon. He will want his wives to have everything prepared.'

Quismah ignored her and continued to cook.

Jalilah offered her hand to Nasir. 'Come. I need you to help me clean the house.' The boy shook his head and scurried out the kitchen.

The Mufraz, or family room, was the most beautifully decorated space in the entire house. Stained glass windows welcomed shards of tinged sunlight into the ornate interior. Pristine cushions lined the walls and an ostentatious rug dominated the centre of the rectangular room.

Nasir sat alone, perched on the edge of an arched window as he played his flute. An engine roared below. He laid his flute down, opened the wooden shutter and leaned out. He watched as a Land Cruiser crunched to a halt outside the front door. Nasir's anxious eyes followed Khalid as he stepped out of the vehicle and entered the house.

Clearly agitated, Nasir rushed to the back of the room and crawled out of an open window. With the agility of a monkey, he clambered down the sheer face of the building. It seemed an impossible feat, but by using projecting gypsum decorations as improvised handholds he quickly reached the ground and raced away.

In the rooftop kitchen, Quismah and Jalilah cooked in a tense silence. Khalid marched in and barked in Arabic at his two wives, 'Why is the food not ready yet?'

Jalilah replied to her irate husband, 'Ask Quismah. I was cleaning your house, husband.'

Khalid glared at Quismah.

'I had to deal with my nephew,' pleaded Quismah.

'Your brother's monkey is of no concern to me,' bawled Khalid. 'He cannot follow the Straight Path. Send him to the wilderness like his accursed father.'

'Husband, it is my duty to look after him,' replied Quismah.

Khalid exploded. 'Silence! It is Allah's will that he goes. Your duty is to serve me.' He grabbed Jalilah's hand. 'At least one of my wives knows how to please me,' he said, dragging Jalilah out of the kitchen.

Quismah screwed up her face in fury and spat into the bubbling rice.

***

The leper sat cross-legged on the ground outside his cave. He picked up a handful of Qat leaves, slipped them under the cloth covering his face and started to chew.

The small bird perched on his shoulder. The leper offered the bird small pieces of grain.

'Eat, my friend. This life is hard and you must eat when you can,' he said in Arabic. The little bird pecked at the grain and chirruped.

Charly's anguished voice spilled out of the cave. 'Ben! For God's sake, run! Quickly! Ben!'

The leper struggled to his feet. The bird fluttered away. He limped into the cave.

Charly was soaked in sweat and delirious. Her fevered head jerked from side to side as she muttered incoherently.

The leper soaked a cloth in a bowl of water and knelt down beside Charly. He gently mopped her brow with the damp cloth and spoke to her quietly. 'What kind of angel are you? Which world are you from?'

The leper traced the dripping cloth along Charly's facial scar, as if his deformed hand was embarked on some strange journey of discovery. 'Have you fallen like me?' he pondered aloud.

The sound of a flute drifted into the cave. The leper's covered head swivelled round. He rose and shuffled outside.

In preparation for his visitor, the leper bent down and collected more stones from the pile at the cave entrance.

Hidden by the trees, Nasir continued to play his flute. The leper launched a stone in the direction of the melancholy sound. The music ceased.

Nasir emerged from the trees. The leper stretched his arm back and threatened to throw again. 'Go! You are not welcome here!' he shouted.

'Please, father. Let me stay. Your sister hates me,' pleaded Nasir.

'No! You cannot,' the leper replied. 'Quismah means well but she is sometimes sad and angry.'

'She is cruel and she beats me,' the young boy cried out.

'If you stay with me, then I will beat you.'

Nasir stole another few steps forward. The leper hurled a large pebble. It thumped into Nasir's chest. The boy was hurt but he refused to cry out. He defiantly wiped away the tears streaming down his cheeks.

'You have let the angel stay with you,' he shouted to his father.

'She is hurt and has no one else.'

'I have no one else. And I found her! She is my angel!' insisted Nasir.

The leper's resistance quickly turned to compassion for his beloved son.

'Go Nasir. Please go, my son.'

Nasir nodded. 'I will come back. Tell the angel I will come back for her with my donkey when she is healed.'

'I will tell her,' the leper promised.

Nasir scurried away. The sound of his flute started to float again through the swaying trees. The leper's sad eyes welled with tears.

***

Ben sat trembling in the corner of his earthen cell. He was still tightly bound with rope.

Tariq, a kindly-looking Arab in his late twenties, squatted opposite Ben. He trained the barrel of his AK47 on his petrified charge.

Ben smacked his parched lips. 'Water,' he uttered in Arabic to his captor.

Tariq grabbed a goatskin water bottle from the floor, jumped to his feet and approached the prisoner. Ben tilted his head back. Tariq angled the bottle over Ben's arid mouth. The water cascaded down his dry throat. Satiated, Ben slumped back. 'Thank you,' he said.

'Are you hungry?' Tariq asked in excellent English. Ben nodded. 'Wait,' commanded Tariq as he headed for the door.

'I'm not going anywhere,' quipped Ben.

Tariq smiled. Ben smiled back. A connection at last.

CHAPTER 10

William Milhouse waited alone on a bench in St James's Park and fiddled with his mobile phone. Frederick Archer strutted up to the bench and sat down. As before, the two men employed the same anti-surveillance drill and avoided direct eye contact.

Both spooks positioned their deactivated phones to their ears and commenced their surreptitious conversation.

'I gather you've seen the news?' asked Archer.

'Yes,' Milhouse replied.

'I would imagine the Americans would call this a 'clusterfuck'. These people are so crude.' A smug smile stretched across Archer's superior face. 'Just like the oil they crave.'

Milhouse braced himself for the inevitable censure.

'Has your man any explanation?' demanded Archer.

'The massacre at the bus wasn't anticipated,' replied Milhouse.

'Nor was the possibility of having a British Army officer running amok in the Yemen wilderness.'

'She's hardly running amok,' said Milhouse.

'She's a war hero and borderline psychopath whose brother has been kidnapped by a group of murderous terrorists. Just give her time. Lawrence of Arabia managed to make a bloody nuisance of himself and he was born in Wales,' thundered Archer.

'She's not Lawrence of Arabia.'

'Quite. She's taller.' Archer paused. 'The PM has just advised me that Special Forces are now involved.' Milhouse winced. Archer continued. 'Messy, I grant you. However we still believe it will have the desired effect. The Yemen Foreign Minister is already hinting at a crackdown on the local bad boys. So I think our colonial cousins across the pond will eventually get their wish.'

'But at what cost?'

'Boys with toys. There's always a price to pay for that type of thing.'

'What price have you paid?' asked Milhouse.

Archer was silenced as a fully-veiled Islamic woman in a black chador and hijab swept past the bench. Her young son toddled behind, kicking a football.

The ball rolled up to Archer's glistening brogues. He smiled at the boy, picked up the football and handed it back. The boy ran off with the ball.

Archer rose leisurely from the bench and spoke into his dead phone. 'Price, you ask? The price every true Englishman has had to pay.' He swung his brolly up as if obeying an order to shoulder arms. 'My man will liaise with yours. Help clean up the mess, et cetera. Can't afford another follow-on. You do understand that, don't you?'

Archer slipped the phone back into his coat pocket and marched away.

***

The guard untied the rope from his prisoner's wrists but left the legs securely trussed. Tariq retreated to his corner of the earthen cell and squatted back down. He trained his gun on Ben and nodded towards a platter of rice and dates on the dirt floor.

'Eat,' Tariq uttered in English.

Ben picked up the platter and wolfed down the food. His eyes flitted between his meal and Tariq's almost-friendly gaze. 'Your English is good,' said Ben.

'I studied in the West.'

'Where?'

Silence. Ben instantly knew he'd made a mistake. He quickly changed the subject. 'I'm a doctor. I came here to help your people.'

'My wife and children were killed by the Americans,' countered Tariq.

'I'm sorry.'

'Can you help me with that?' asked Tariq angrily.

'If you release me, I can help you find justice.'

Tariq exploded. 'Justice! There is only one kind of justice you people in the West understand.'

'But I'm on your side,' said Ben.

Tariq shook his head. 'If we release you, you will tell the Americans who we are and where we are.'

'No. No, I wouldn't,' said Ben, desperately. 'I don't even know who you are.'

'You do. You have no hood.'

'But you took the hood off.'

Tariq maintained an ominous silence. Ben's face filled with dread as his fate finally began to become clear.

***

A flickering oil lamp illuminated the gloomy cave and cast dancing shadows on the walls of the ancient rock. It was if prehistoric cave paintings had come to life.

The leper knelt beside Charly and cupped some water into her mouth. She stirred and her eyes fluttered open. The fever had broken.

Charly looked up at the leper's covered face and gazed into his dark eyes. Stripped of eyelashes, they looked like pieces of coal floating on a sea of cotton. For a few fuzzy moments, Charly didn't know whether she was awake or still dreaming. Then her parched mouth slowly started to move. 'God's peace be upon you,' she uttered in Arabic. The leper didn't respond. Maybe she *was* dreaming, she thought. Her eyes struggled to focus in the poor light as she tried again. 'Where am I?' she asked.

'You are safe,' the leper replied in perfect English.

'You speak English?' said Charly, sounding surprised.

'And you speak Arabic,' the leper replied. He paused. 'Are you an angel?'

Charly appeared confused. 'What?'

'My son thinks you are an angel.'

Charly shook her head but her mind started to swim. 'No. I'm no angel. My name is Charlotte. My friends...' she hesitated, 'my friends call me Charly.'

'Then I will call you Charly,' said the leper.

Charly's eyes darted about the cave. 'How long have I been here?'

'Four days. But your fever has gone.'

Charly struggled to raise herself up but the effort was too much and she flopped back down. She coughed and grimaced as pain seared through her tender shoulder.

'I took the bullet out. Your wound is healing,' said the leper.

Charley became agitated. 'I must get help for my brother. He has been kidnapped by terrorists.'

'Is he a spy?'

'No.'

'Are you a spy?'

Charly hesitated. 'No. No, my brother is a doctor. I am a nurse. We came with medical supplies for the people of Yemen. We were ambushed. He was captured but I got away.'

'Who did this?' asked the leper.

'A group of Yemeni men. Their leader wore a black eye-patch.'

Charly's gaze followed the leper as he stood up and hobbled towards a long wooden box in a corner of the cave. He took a key, which was hanging from a piece of twine around his neck, then bent over and opened the padlock which secured the box. The leper lifted the lid of the long container and reached in. He hauled out an AK47, clipped a magazine into the weapon and rested it against the cave wall. He then locked the box and turned to Charly. 'You must eat.'

'I'm not hungry,' she replied.

The leper picked up a large plate of rice, dates and meat from the cave floor and handed it to Charly. 'You are still weak. Eat.'

Charly took the plate and picked at the food. The leper grabbed the AK47 and shuffled out of the cave.

Charly was sleeping on her back, covered with a blanket. She jerked awake. Disorientated, she squinted around the cave for a few moments.

She eased herself up from the floor, stretched, then limped unsteadily to the mouth of the cave.

The leper sat cross-legged beside the smoking campfire. A bowl of green Qat leaves lay by his side. The cloth concealing his face rippled up and down as he chewed the leaves. The small bird fluttered down and perched on his arm. He whispered to it in Arabic. 'How are you today my little friend?' He held up pieces of rice to the bird's tiny beak as it pecked away.

Leaning against a wall by the cave entrance, Charly observed the leper feeding the bird. Catching the sensitivity of this mysterious stranger, she smiled. 'I have to leave and get help,' she said quietly in English.

The leper's covered head swivelled round. 'Charly! You are stronger. Yes?' He pointed to the campfire. 'Sit. I will make you tea and honey.'

Charly eased herself down beside the fire. The leper wafted his arm and the little bird flew off. He rose to his feet and hobbled to the primitive well to draw water for the tea.

Charly and the leper sat around the campfire, drinking tea from small clay tumblers and eating combs of honey.

'The honey's good,' said Charly.

'This part of the Yemen is famous for its honey. I have my own hives in the valley.' The leper paused, as if considering whether or not to ask his question. 'You have a husband?'

'No,' replied an awkward-looking Charly.

'This honey will make you want a husband. And when he is tired, the honey will make him want to be with you. And to make babies.'

'I think I'd need a lot of honey to want a husband.'

'Why say this? You are young and pretty. You are strong!'

'Western men don't like their women to be strong.'

'In Yemen, women need to be strong. Life is hard here.'

'Life is also hard for women in the West. And our men make it harder.'

The leper contemplated for a moment. 'I think you are right, Charly,' he said. 'You will need a lot of honey.'

She chuckled and shook her head. The small bird flew down and landed on the leper's shoulder. Charly stared at the bird. ' It likes you,' she said.

'He was injured by a hawk and I made him well. We are friends.'

'Must be a habit of yours,' she said, smiling. 'I remember a boy. He helped me…'

The leper nodded. 'That was my son, Nasir. He found you and brought you here on his donkey.'

'He saved my life. I owe him.' She looked around. 'Where is he?'

The leper pointed down the mountainside. 'He lives with my sister in the valley.'

Charly glimpsed his exposed claw-like hand. The leper caught her look and quickly covered up the deformity.

'And your wife?' she asked.

'She is dead.'

There was silence for a few moments.

'There is medication that can help you be with your son,' said Charly.

'There is nothing that can help me,' said the leper, with real bitterness in his voice.

He stood and limped towards the cave entrance, then halted. He slowly turned and faced Charly. 'How will you save your brother?' he asked.

Charly stared into the smouldering campfire for a few seconds. This was certainly a question that needed to be answered. 'I don't know. But I'll find a way,' she eventually replied.

'I know you will. Angels always find a way,' said the leper. And with that, he shuffled into the cave.

The leper stood in the gloom, staring down at the long wooden box. He crouched over and unlocked it. He pushed aside the AK47 to reveal a pile of neatly stacked photographs.

He picked up the first small photograph and studied it. Staring back at the leper was the portrait of a beautiful Arabic woman in her twenties wearing a head scarf. The leper traced a misshapen finger around the image of the woman's face; just in the same way he had followed the ragged edge of Charly's scar. Tears spilled from the leper's eyes and soaked into the cloth wrapped around his face. He gazed at his wife's beautiful face and whispered to her in Arabic, 'Allah has sent me an angel.'

CHAPTER 11

Tariq squatted in a corner of the cell and pointed his gun at Ben. His prisoner grimaced and moaned with pain. A concerned-looking Tariq stood up.

'What is wrong?' he asked Ben in English.

'I must go to the toilet.'

Tariq picked up a bucket and threw it at Ben.

'I can't,' Ben protested. 'It's my bowels. I promise you, I won't try to escape.'

Tariq pondered for a few seconds. He took out a knife from his belt and approached his captive. Ben reared back in fear. Tariq bent down and cut the rope which bound Ben's legs. He took a step back and pointed his AK47 at the prisoner's chest. 'Get up. If you run, I will shoot.'

Ben struggled to his feet. He was unsteady and paused for the circulation to return to his lower limbs.

Tariq unlocked the door then gestured to Ben with the gun muzzle. Ben shuffled out the mud shack, followed by Tariq.

Ben's eyes squinted as he tried to make out the features of what appeared to be a mud-brick compound. The sound of bleating goats permeated the oppressive darkness.

Tariq nudged Ben in the back with his gun. 'Go to these bushes,' he ordered.

The two men walked to some shrubs lining the edge of the compound. Ben's eyes darted about as he scanned the gloomy terrain. The compound appeared empty. He knew this would be his only chance.

Ben reached a large thorn bush. Tariq nodded towards it. 'In there. Be quick.'

Tariq scrutinized Ben as he squeezed himself through the prickly bush into a small clearing. He dropped his trousers, squatted down and grunted with the apparent effort of trying to force out a shit. An embarrassed Tariq looked on, still training his AK47 on his constipated prisoner.

Somewhere in the darkness, a dog barked. Tariq instinctively wheeled round and squinted through the inky blackness in an effort to locate the cause of the disturbance. He could see nothing so turned back and peered into the bush. No squatting figure! He brushed the thorny twigs away with the barrel of his gun. There was no Ben. The prisoner had escaped.

Ben sprinted through the pitch blackness. Twigs and thorns whipped his body and lacerated his skin as he raced past unseen trees and bushes. He could hear the raised voices of alarm behind him followed by the thud of pursuing feet. But he didn't look back. He just panted for air and kept running.

In the mud brick compound, an agitated terrorist ran up to Tariq. 'We'd better catch him before Khalid finds out,' he screamed.

A Land Cruiser swerved into the compound. Terrorists piled into the back of the vehicle. Above the driver's cabin, a powerful searchlight exploded into life. The laden vehicle roared into the bushes after Ben.

The chasing Cruiser bumped and rattled through the brush, its floodlight penetrating the darkness like a white-hot laser.

An exhausted Ben could hear the growl of an engine gaining ground on him, stalking him like a predatory beast. He kept running. He had no choice.

A terrorist in the rear of the vehicle guided the unforgiving light beam as it sliced through the bushes and trees like an enormous sabre. Ben glanced back. They were nearly on him; maybe only thirty feet away. He dug deeper but his tank was nearly empty.

Then the searchlight irradiated Ben. Terrorists screamed out. Ben stumbled and fell onto one knee. He struggled up, but it was too late. The Cruiser was only feet away. Game over.

A massive bang sounded in the darkness. The Land Cruiser somersaulted in the air, crashed into the dirt and slewed to halt. Ben looked back and saw the crumpled vehicle. Steam hissed from the racing engine but there was no sign of his pursuers. For a man who harboured no belief in a God, Ben was prepared to accept this apparent sign of Divine Intervention. He laughed a manic laugh and sprinted away. Towards freedom.

***

The chill of the dawn was sharp. Ben had been running for what seemed like hours and the sweat covering his body felt as if it had transformed into a thin film of ice. His face, torso and limbs were shredded and covered with dried rivulets of blood. He shivered as he cowered behind a tree at the edge of a dirt road.

A faint engine noise cut through the early morning stillness. Ben staggered onto the road and peered into the distance. He saw a car bumping along the rutted road in a cloud of dust. It wasn't a Land Cruiser and looked as if it contained only one occupant; so no terrorists, he assumed.

Ben took his chance and frantically waved his arms in front of the approaching vehicle. The car sped straight towards Ben, its tyres churning up the sandy ground. He kept waving but the car kept accelerating. Ben stood his ground but the car wasn't going to stop. At the last moment, Ben dived to the side of the road and the car flashed past in a swirl of dust.

Sprawled in the dirt, Ben began to sob like an infant. He was totally broken. Then he heard the sound of braking and raised his head. The car was reversing. His despair turned to joy.

Ben scrambled to his feet and flagged the car down. 'Thank you! Thank you!' he gasped.

The car finally stopped. A smiling Ben tapped on the roof and the driver stepped out. Ben stared at the Arabic man in disbelief. It was the hotel manager; the man who had betrayed Ben and Charly after the terrorist ambush. The manager pointed an AK47 at his horrified captive.

Ben rushed at him and grappled with the gun. But he was too weak. The manager shoved Ben to the ground and battered him on the head with the butt of his gun. Ben slumped unconscious, face down, into the dirt. He was a hostage again.

An armed and impatient Khalid stood waiting with his men in the mud brick compound.

In the middle of the group, a nervous Tariq fidgeted with his AK47.

A car raced into the compound and stopped beside the assembled terrorists. The manager stepped out of the dusty vehicle and greeted Khalid in Arabic. 'God's peace be upon you.'

'And God's peace be upon you,' Khalid replied.

The manager popped open his car boot. Khalid peered inside. Ben lay cowering in the cramped space. He was bound and covered in blood and his eyes started to blink as the harsh light flooded in.

Khalid smiled and handed a wad of US Dollars to the manager. 'Buy another hotel,' he quipped.

Two of Khalid's men hauled Ben out of the boot and bundled him onto the ground. The hotel manager jumped into his car and drove off.

Khalid approached his prostrate hostage. He looked down at Ben and spoke to him for the first time in English. 'Watch.'

Ben glanced up at Khalid and dreaded what was about to happen next.

Khalid stared hard at his men. They tried to avoid eye contact with their leader, as if his lethal gaze had the power to turn each of them to stone.

'Who let the Infidel escape?' barked Khalid in Arabic. Tariq appeared uneasy but none of the men spoke. 'Who?' Khalid screamed again.

The terrified men remained silent.

Then Tariq stepped forward. 'It was me,' he said.

Khalid threw him a disarming smile then admonished his men. 'So at least there is one man amongst you who is not a coward.' Tariq started to visibly relax. Khalid patted him on the shoulder and spoke quietly. 'I will tell your father you died with honour.'

A look of panic filled Tariq's face. He fumbled with his gun but it was too late. Khalid's AK47 thundered in retribution. The bullets tore into Tariq's chest and his lifeless body crumpled to the ground.

Khalid's men watched in horrified silence. No one dared to move.

Khalid bawled out his order. 'It is not safe here. Take the Infidel to the other compound. It will soon be time.'

Ben lay on the ground and whimpered. He now knew his fate. It was unavoidable. All the miracles in the world weren't going to save him now.

CHAPTER 12

Charly emerged from the cave in her bare feet. She was stripped to her soiled pants and ripped T-shirt. She glanced around. There was no sign of the leper.

She sat on the ground, lay back and commenced a gruelling series of sit-ups. Her face winced with pain as muscle fibres already weakened by trauma stretched to breaking point. It felt like her whole body was on fire.

After an agonising twenty minutes, Charly issued a deep groan and lay exhausted on the ground.

The leper trekked up the rocky slope towards his cave. A dead mountain hare bobbled about on his shoulder as he slowly picked his way through the boulders and scree. He reached the treeline and stopped. Through the foliage he spotted Charly breathing heavily on the ground; flat on her stomach, arms by her sides. He watched in silence as she started her push-ups. With gritted teeth, she battled to raise her ravaged body off the ground. Her arms vibrated with the effort but she couldn't do it. She was too weak and the pain was unendurable. Screaming with frustration, she collapsed face-first into the dirt.

The leper studied Charly's spent body. His dark, brooding eyes surveyed her strong arms and muscled shoulders. He was impressed by her taut stomach which appeared as unyielding as the surrounding rock. But above all else, he was captivated by her golden hair, paler than the honey he harvested, but brighter than any midday sun.

The leper stood – transfixed – luxuriating in the image of his angel until she eventually scrambled up from the dirt and padded back to the cave.

***

Frederick Archer stood immersed in a crowd. He was in London Zoo, observing the antics of his relations on display in the monkey enclosure.

The onlookers pointed and laughed as the screeching primates bounded and darted about.

William Milhouse edged his way slowly through the throng and stopped beside Archer. The two men engaged in a stealthy conversation. At no point did either man acknowledge the other's presence.

'Things are out of control,' said a worried-looking Milhouse.

'Things?' queried Archer.

'Our outside contractor wishes to revise the terms.'

Archer's eyes followed the frenetic monkeys. 'Does he indeed. In what way?'

'He insists that the product is despatched in full before the agreed completion date.'

Archer's superior smile dissolved. Yet he seemed, on the surface, unruffled. After all, appearances were everything in his line of business.

'What do you see when you look into that monkey cage?' Archer asked.

Milhouse stared at the hyperactive primates; fighting, howling, grunting. But he remained silent.

Archer continued. 'It's bedlam. Utter chaos. But there is a system. And the fittest will always survive.' Archer paused for effect. 'Restore control. Now. Do that and your product will be unscathed, fit for purpose and delivered on time.'

'And if I can't?' asked Milhouse.

There was a slight twitch of Archer's head and Milhouse thought he could hear him tutting. Archer eventually delivered his answer. 'Then some of us may go permanently out of business.' His smile returned. 'It's a dog-eat-dog world out there. One must always maintain a competitive edge. Or face the consequences.'

Archer glided away slowly through the crowd like a ghost.

A monkey clattered up to the front bars of the enclosure and screeched. Milhouse flinched. He stared at the gurning primate for a few seconds. His nostrils flared at the rancid scent of the beast's breath. Eventually, he eased his way back through – what felt like to him – an ogling and pathetic mass of humanity.

***

Two days later, Charly resumed her gruelling struggle with fitness. Sucking up the pain, she was now able to execute the challenging push-ups. Her rigid, horizontal body now soared from the earth and dropped back down with rhythmic ease. Sweat from her brow spattered onto the sand like droplets of life-giving rain. She was back.

The leper hoisted the pulley from his primitive well and filled a bucket with fresh spring water. As he returned to the cave with the bucket, he stopped and observed Charly's workout. He could only assume that, for all their virtues, angels were also mad.

'Are all nurses in the West like you?' he asked Charly in English.

Continuing to pump herself up and down, a breathless Charly replied. 'We like to keep fit.' After a few more repetitions she continued, 'I'm going to find my brother now.'

'I will make a fire,' said the leper.

***

Charly sat gazing into the campfire. She rubbed her aching shoulder and winced with pain.

The leper emerged from the cave. 'Come, Charly. I take you to my bees,' he said smiling.

'I told you,' she replied. 'I'm going to find my brother.'

The leper contemplated for a few moments. 'There is a Yemen army checkpoint in the valley. Close to my bee hives.'

'Is it far?'

'Everywhere in Yemen is far,' said the leper, nodding. 'But you need more honey. It will make you well.'

'Will I be able to see the village in the valley?'

'You think your brother is held there?'

'Don't you?' snapped Charly.

The leper ignored Charly's rhetorical question. He stared at her grimy Western clothing.

'You need to change,' he said.

***

The epic scale of the territory was marked by vertiginous cliffs and sheer rock walls which towered above a crumbling volcanic slope. However, it was a barren landscape, interrupted only by the occasional shrub and skeletal tree.

With the AK47 slung over his shoulder, the leper carefully picked his way down the unstable scree. Charly followed, now fully robed and wearing a turban. Her alert eyes flashed about as she reconnoitred the terrain; preparing herself for what she would soon have to do.

'Be careful. Don't fall,' said the leper, as he glanced back at Charly. She nodded as they continued their precarious descent.

After another twenty minutes, Charly halted. She gazed down into the valley. The sight was both spectacular and ruggedly beautiful. Terraced slopes had been neatly etched out of the mountainside and their crops of maize and millet rippled in the light breeze. Wadis, gouged out of the valley floor, resembled an unending network of stone capillaries awaiting the infusion of life-sustaining floodwater.

Charly soon spotted the distant village. It nestled into the valley plain, as if for sanctuary, and was surrounded by ancient fortified walls. Scattered within the walls were whitewashed and redbrick houses. Charly peered closer and saw the green-domed Mosque with its crescent symbol which marked the epicentre of the settlement. There was no doubt; she was in the land of Mahomet.

Charly turned to the leper and pointed. 'Is that Nasir's village?' He nodded.

After another hour they were hiking along a flat sandy plain. They had left the cool mountain air behind them and were both starting to sweat in the hotter, dryer conditions. This area was largely featureless and the burning sun beat down on the two travellers. Only swaying palm and almond trees offered the promise of shade.

The leper led Charly through an avenue of flowering Al-sidr and Acacia trees. He stopped and pointed. 'This is where my bees like to feed.'

Hundreds of small dark bees buzzed and darted around the leper's hive boxes. Charley watched them with delight and smiled. The leper stroked one of the ancient hives with his covered hand. 'This is their home,' he said proudly.

'It's not what I expected,' said Charly, looking surprised. 'In the West, hives are very different.'

'I think many things are different in the West,' he said.

The leper led Charly to the rear of the log hive. He drove his hand through the mud seal and pulled out a honeycomb. 'Taste,' he said, handing it to Charly.

'It's delicious,' she exclaimed as she licked the honey.

'We rest now. Then I take you to the checkpoint.'

The pair sat cross-legged on the ground beside the hives. They observed in silence as the industrious bees continued to swarm in and out of their honey factories.

The leper eventually spoke. 'The bees know it is not good to be alone. They live and work together. As one.' He paused, then looked directly at Charly. 'They make the honey to sweeten your heart, Charly.'

Charly picked up a stone and rolled it around her hand. 'My heart?' she mumbled. After a few seconds of contemplation, she continued. 'Does no one steal your honey?'

The leper shook his head. 'The people in this valley don't know where I live but they know this is my honey.' He issued a throaty chuckle. 'And I think if this was your honey, they would not eat it.'

Charly forced a smile but inside she felt hurt. Despite everything, she wanted the leper to like her and to think of her as a woman. Christ, even 'harlot' was a label she'd willingly accept. But it seemed as if he was the same as all the others. She was a harridan, and the term had obviously gone global. And to add insult to injury, she was now the 'honey monster'.

Charly stared down at the dusty ground and drew a line in the sand with her finger. Lines were all she ever drew. Borders to define and protect. Frontiers which must never be crossed. All invaders had to be repelled and Charly was good at that.

Then the unsolicited memories came flooding back. She kept tapping the ground with her finger as she spoke, as if trying to use Morse Code to communicate with a painful past. 'My mother abandoned me when I was a baby. I've always wondered how she could do that. Walk away from her child.'

'That is hard, but sometimes a parent has no choice,' said the leper. He paused. 'Have you always been on your own?'

'In a way, I suppose,' Charly replied. 'I had parents who adopted me and my brother but…Ben's all I've got left. Seven billion people on the planet and it's just me and him.'

'And the bees,' said the leper.

'And the bees,' said Charly, smiling. 'Tell me about your wife,' she asked.

'My wife was a beautiful woman,' the leper replied. He turned to Charly. 'Just like you.' He hesitated for a moment, as if trying to order scrambled memories in his brain. 'I had a good job, teaching English. We were very happy.' His hoarse voice faltered. 'But then she died. Giving birth to our second child. They both died. This is common in Yemen.' The leper paused again, fighting the emotion welling up inside. He pointed at the bees thrumming around the logs. 'I became angry,' he said. ' Sometimes the bees become angry. That's when they sting. And die.'

'What was your wife's name?' asked Charly.

'Hala,' he whispered.

'I know that name,' she said. 'It means sweetness.'

The leper slowly nodded his head and sat quietly for a few minutes. Then he rose stiffly to his feet and offered Charly his hand. 'Come. I take you to the checkpoint.'

CHAPTER 13

Aden was scorching hot.

Ahmed ambled out of an opulent glass building. It was the Aden headquarters of Carrington Trust Petroleum.

Colin Smith occupied the driver's seat of a hired jeep and watched Ahmed cross the road towards an SUV. Smith had gone native and was wearing a local turban and wraparound skirt. Large sunglasses covered his hawk-like eyes.

Ahmed stepped into his SUV and accelerated into traffic. Smith gunned his jeep in pursuit. The SUV weaved through the bustling streets, covertly followed by Smith's jeep.

Thirty minutes later, Ahmed was now driving on an empty desert road. He peered through his dusty windscreen - as if looking for something, or someone. A Land Cruiser was parked fifty yards up the road. Ahmed braked and slowed to a stop behind the stationary vehicle.

Smith's jeep sped past the two vehicles and drove another few hundred yards before stopping. He adjusted his rear view mirror and watched. He could see Ahmed step out of the SUV. An Arabic figure stepped out of the Land Cruiser. Smith reached across to the passenger seat and grabbed a camera with a long telephoto lens.

Smith stepped out of the jeep with his camera and stared into the distance. He could see Ahmed was talking to the man. Smith's eyes narrowed as he tried to make out more detail. The man was wearing an eye-patch. It was Khalid.

Smith headed towards some trees by the side of the road. Using them as cover, he moved closer to the two men then stopped. He leaned against a tree and pointed his camera at the two talking heads. Click! He took a photograph. Click! Then another. The camera continued to click as Smith observed and photographed his targets.

Staring through his powerful lens, Smith could tell Ahmed was shouting. Then he saw Khalid slap him. Ahmed staggered back and reached for his dagger but Khalid punched him and he crumpled in a heap.

Smith could see the altercation was intensifying. Khalid pulled an AK47 from his Land Cruiser and loomed over a cowering Ahmed. It looked as if he was about to shoot him but he hesitated. After a tense standoff, Khalid spat on Ahmed, turned and jumped back into his vehicle.

A shaken Ahmed struggled to his feet and ran to his SUV.

Smith hid behind the tree as Khalid's Land Cruiser flashed past. He then sprinted to his jeep, circled it on the sandy road and drove back towards the SUV.

Ahmed sat in the safety of his vehicle. His hands trembled as he prepared to make a call on his mobile. The car door opened. A petrified Ahmed dropped his phone and struggled in vain to pull the door shut. He looked up and saw the looming figure of Colin Smith.

Smith lit a fag then offered one to Ahmed. The Arab shook his head.

'Friend of yours?' asked Smith. Ahmed nodded his head. Smith smiled. 'Looked a bit touchy. Must be difficult for a one-eyed man to see both sides of the argument.'

'I saw you at the airport,' said Ahmed.

'Everyone needs a holiday. Sun. Sea. Fucking sand. Everywhere. Nothing but fucking sand. What else would a fun-loving spook want?'

'Why are you here?'

Smith sniggered. 'Christ! Tell me you didn't just ask me that.'

'Did Milhouse send you?' asked Ahmed nervously.

Smith's snigger quickly morphed into a belly laugh. 'Milhouse?' Then his face turned to stone in an instant. 'This whole thing needs re-engineered.'

'I don't know what you are talking about,' said Ahmed, looking confused.

'Don't worry. You soon will. Rules of this particular game have changed as of now. You're going to make friends again with Captain Cyclops and everyone's going to be happy.'

'I can't…' Ahmed protested.

Smith battered the door window with his fist. 'Don't. Do not say another word. Just listen.'

***

A dark green Saudi Arabian flag fluttered above the heavily fortified complex. Armed sentries in watchtowers keenly observed the surrounding desert terrain. The heat was intense and inescapable. This was the Saudi/Yemen border and it was a hot spot in more ways than one.

A solitary light bulb illuminated a small, featureless room in the bowels of the Saudi fort. Four tough looking British men in desert fatigues stood in conference. It was Captain Anderson and his elite Special Forces team. The best of the best. Or the worst of the worst, depending on which side you were on.

None of the men were particularly tall or broad. For some reason, Special Forces seemed to favour the small and compact – presumably confirming a preference towards the size of the fight in the man rather than the size of the man in the fight.

Jock was the stockiest. Face hewn from Aberdeen granite, he was the joker in the pack. Always the one for light relief when the chips were down, or completely obliterated.

Paddy was lean and taciturn, with a stern face unused to smiling. So not really a party animal as such. Just an animal.

Robbo twirled a lethal commando dagger around his surprisingly delicate paw. Apparently distracted, but taking it all in.

Captain Anderson jabbed a finger onto a wall map. 'This is our Infill point. Twenty-two hundred hours.'

'Method?' asked Robbo.

'Chopper,' replied the Captain.

Jock glanced at Paddy. 'Christ! You'd better take your travel sickness pills ya fucking fanny!' Unamused, Paddy glowered back.

The Captain tapped on the map a second time. 'Intel confirms this is where he's being held. He was moved here seventy-two hours ago.'

'How reliable?' asked Paddy.

'Spook sighting. Man on the inside apparently.'

Robbo shook his shaved head, still twirling the dagger. He resembled the botched outcome of a laboratory experiment involving a pit-bull and a mountain gorilla. 'This reeks of shit!' he said.

The Captain ignored Robbo's comment and rigidly adhered to the script. 'This one's time sensitive,' he told his men. 'So we don't have the luxury of an extended OP. We TAB in, get our hostage, kill the bad guys and make for the ERV point by twenty-two hundred hours.'

Paddy looked uneasy. 'If we don't eyeball, we're working blind. Surely we need to set up an OP and see what we're dealing with. The hostage might not be there. It could be an ambush.'

'Not an option,' said the Captain. 'Apparently, our source has confirmed that the bad guys are planning a Halal film spectacular tonight. Our man's the star attraction. The butcher's knife has already been sharpened. It's a 'GO'.'

'What's our man's name?' asked Jock.

'Ben Stevens,' replied the Captain. 'He was with his sister but she somehow managed to evade the kidnappers. Best guess is that she's running loose on the ground.'

'Christ, she's not going to fuck things up, is she?' said Paddy, frowning.

The Captain shook his head. 'No. She's off the radar. And she's one of us. Won the MC in Afghanistan. Her father's a posthumous VC. Mount Tumbledown.'

'That's a lot of hardware for one family. They must be popular at Car Boot sales,' quipped Jock.

After a wry grin, the Captain locked eye contact with his men. 'Right. Let's do it.'

***

The leper and Charly tramped along the valley plain. He stopped and pointed towards a small mud hut at the side of a rutted dirt track. 'That is the Checkpoint but I see no soldiers. You stay here. I will go.'

Charly seemed unconvinced. 'It doesn't look like a checkpoint.'

The leper readied his AK47 and advanced towards the hut.

Charly observed as he entered the hut. A few seconds later, he re-emerged and stood still as his black eyes scanned the barren surroundings.

The leper limped back to Charly. 'They have gone. Or been taken.'

'Taken?'

'The army is not popular in this valley.'

Charly became increasingly agitated. She started pacing up and down like a caged animal. 'Look. I need to get help for my brother. Which way do I go?'

The leper shook his head. 'It is not safe for you here. You will not get out of this valley alive on foot.'

This wasn't what Charly wanted to hear. She had to leave. Now! 'Can you give me your AK47?' she blurted out.

The leper's mood changed in a heartbeat. He glanced at his weapon then glared suspiciously at Charly. 'If you are a nurse, then how do you know how to use this?'

Charly knew she had made a mistake. A big one. Fucking typical, she thought. Here she was, lost in the middle of Arabia, and to top it all, she'd let the fucking genie out of the bottle. All she could do was stutter. 'I don't…it's just that…'

'Are you a spy, Charly?' the leper spat out aggressively. 'Have you come to harm my people?'

'No! Of course not. I just want to save my brother.'

The leper cocked his AK47. 'We need to get back. It will be dark soon.' He pointed the weapon at Charly. 'You go first. I will follow.'

Charly stared hard at the leper. It was clear a gulf of mistrust had opened up between them. For the first time she began to think of the leper, not as her saviour, but as an enemy. And that hurt deep inside. She was quickly running out of any sentient beings on the planet who might actually give a fuck about whether she lived or died. That's why she had to find Ben. He seemed to be the only person in this shit-filled world who validated her existence with his unconditional love. And for that, she loved him dearly in return. He would be saved. He MUST be saved. And she would be the one to do it.

'Move!' barked the leper.

Charly shook her head in exasperation and reluctantly trudged back towards the mountain.

CHAPTER 14

Another kidnap room. Deliberately anonymous-looking with black cloth draped over the walls. There was no visual evidence of where this lair might be located – and that was exactly the point.

Ben sat slouched on the earthen floor, now wearing a bright orange boiler suit; the uniform of impending slaughter. He was bruised and broken and his hands and feet were shackled with medieval-looking chains.

An armed guard sat opposite Ben, pointing an AK47 at his chest.

Ben's mouth was so dry with thirst and fear that he could hardly swallow. 'Water?' he asked his guard in Arabic.

The guard stood and walked over. He spat in Ben's face. 'Drink this,' he shouted at Ben. 'Tonight we kill you like an animal.' The smirking guard bleated like a goat and drew his finger across his throat.

Ben's head drooped with despair. A cockroach scuttled over his manacled legs. He squirmed on the floor and screamed.

The guard laughed.

***

It was night.

The Special Forces helicopter had reached the Infill point and a small dust storm churned up beneath the swirling rotors.

Enormous tendrils seemed to sprout from the belly of the hovering chopper. They squirmed like snakes in the downdraft.

Captain Anderson and his three-man team abseiled down the dangling ropes onto the sandy plain. They were wearing full combat gear and laden with heavy bergens.

When his men were clear, the Captain looked up and circled with his gloved hand. The helicopter tilted to its left and disappeared into the blackness. The swirling dust was quickly becalmed.

The four soldiers marched silently through the night in single file; infra-red goggles secured around their camouflaged faces.

Captain Anderson and Jock carried M16 assault rifles. Both with M203 grenade launchers attached.

Paddy cradled an L96 A1 sniper rifle with night sight.

Robbo was on point, wielding a Minimi light machine gun.

The warriors advanced below the ridge line, expertly blending in with the surrounding desert landscape.

Islamic banners of war now covered the walls of Ben's new cell. A dramatic backdrop for the imminent filmed 'event'.

Khalid and four masked terrorists circled their prisoner as he knelt on a large polythene sheet draped across the floor. Ben knew what this meant and he quivered with primal fear.

In an opposite corner of the earthen cell, an unmasked terrorist filmed the proceedings with a Camcorder.

Khalid manoeuvred behind Ben, glared into the Camcorder and started to rant in Arabic. 'Kafirs of the West. The fire is already lit and is just awaiting the wind. The might of Allah will crush you and your families and you will crumble like the accursed towers of America. Behold. This is the wrath of Allah which awaits you all.'

The Special Forces team stealthily approached a mud-brick compound. They halted.

Captain Anderson checked his GPS device then signalled with his hand for the team to advance.

The soldiers moved into the deserted compound. The Captain raised his hand and pointed to a small mud hut. They crept towards it. Twenty yards. Fifteen yards. Ten yards. They stopped.

He and Jock fitted gas masks as Paddy and Robbo covered them with a potential three hundred and sixty degree arc of fire.

The two masked soldiers moved silently to the front door of the hut.

Paddy and Robbo took flanking positions on either side. They crouched by the windows, gas canisters and stun grenades in hand.

Khalid's eyes burned with hatred as he concluded his manic polemic to camera. 'God is great and Muhammad is his prophet. Praise Allah! Praise God! Praise him! It is the will of God!'

Khalid's men screamed out, 'Allahu Akbar! Allahu Akbar!'

Ben was hysterical. He pleaded for his life in English. 'Please don't do this! I beg you! I came here to help your people. I am not a spy!'

Khalid drew a large razor-sharp knife from his camouflage jacket, grabbed Ben's hair and yanked his head back.

The Camcorder kept filming as Ben screamed in terror.

Paddy and Robbo battered open the wooden window shutters with their weapons and hurled gas canisters and stun grenades into the hut.

Captain Anderson kicked open the front door and rushed inside, quickly followed by Jock. Their red gun lasers cut and darted through the smoke-filled room. The Captain screamed through his gas mask. 'Ben! On the floor! On the floor now!'

Both soldiers searched the hut thoroughly. But it was empty. Ben had been moved.

The hyper terrorists continued to chant. 'Allahu Akbar! Allahu Akbar!'

Ben could feel the cold sharpness of a blade slice into his Adam's apple. The terror was paralyzing as he clamped his eyes shut and felt the pain sear through his body.

Khalid started to saw through his prisoner's windpipe. Blood spurted from Ben's neck and a horrible gurgling sound escaped from his butchered throat. Without mercy, Khalid continued to cut and hack.

Once the grotesque deed was done, a triumphant Khalid raised Ben's decapitated head aloft. Blood streamed down his arm and dripped onto the polythene sheet as he shrieked into the Camcorder. 'Behold! This is the fate of all Crusaders and Infidels!'

***

A ghastly scream reverberated around the cave. The leper jolted awake. He squinted across at Charly. Through the faint light of an oil lamp, he could see she was mumbling and writhing on the ground in a cold sweat. Still asleep, she was clearly gripped by a terrible nightmare.

The leper hobbled across to Charly. He knelt down and gently shook her agitated body. She jerked awake, looking confused and panicked.

The leper whispered to her in English. 'Charly, what is wrong?'

Charly hugged the leper tightly and sobbed into his chest. He stroked her matted hair.

'Something's happened to my brother,' she cried. 'I must go to him now.'
'It is just a bad dream. You need to rest. We will talk in the morning.'
Charly continued to weep as the leper cradled her in his arms.

***

Outside the empty hut, Captain Anderson wrenched off his gas mask and spoke calmly into his radio. 'Target empty. Buzzard has flown with prey. Repeat. Target empty. Buzzard has flown with prey. Over.'

A flare swished into the night sky and burst into a shower of incandescent phosphorous. The Captain and his men were bathed in a dazzling light.

Gun barrels glowed orange in the darkness as the staccato of heavy gunfire crackled from all sides of the compound.

A hail of bullets zipped past the Special Forces team like angry hornets. 'Contact front and sides! Fan out and fire. One hundred and eighty degree arc,' yelled the Captain to his men.

Robbo opened up with the Minimi machine gun. With a deafening RAT-A-TAT-A-TAT the bullets spat out of the thirty round magazine and peppered the surrounding buildings.

A heavy rate of incoming fire thundered from a small shack to the soldiers' left. Jock launched an M203 grenade. It roared into the shack and exploded in a raging fireball.

As the overhead flare faded, the incoming fire intensified from all sides.

'Withdraw!' shouted the Captain.

The team pulled back in two pairs, covering each other and firing ferociously.

An RPG sliced through the darkness and slammed into Robbo, eviscerating his upper torso. Charred body parts flew past his battling comrades.

The Captain, Paddy and Jock maintained their disciplined retreat. No panic. Just controlled but aggressive salvos towards their unseen assailants.

Gunfire crackled from another shack. Paddy's head snapped back as a bullet drilled through his brain. He crumpled, lifeless, to the ground.

Captain Anderson launched a grenade. It roared into the fragile shack and exploded. A screaming man in flames staggered out of the conflagration. He collapsed and writhed in the dirt. The Captain finished him off with his M16.

He and Jock were now at the edge of the compound; only feet away from the comparative safety of the pitch black wilderness.

A hand grenade spiralled through the air and clattered on the ground beside Jock. He tried to grab it but it was too late. The explosion killed the Scotsman instantly. White-hot shrapnel ripped into Captain Anderson's legs. The muscles and tendons of his shredded limbs hung out of his perforated trousers like pieces of sliced octopus. He groaned and slumped to the ground.

The Captain crawled along the dirt towards the sanctuary of a goat pen. His mind was fuzzy but he could hear the bleating of the panicked animals.

Tiny dust bowls flew up as bullets ricocheted off the ground around the scrambling soldier. His unfocussed eyes remained fixed on the pen as dragged himself forward.

The Captain grimaced in pain as a bullet smashed into his side, tearing flesh and splintering bone. But he kept going. Inching himself towards cover. Dragging his weapon with him as he crawled along the sand.

Panting heavily, he finally reached the goat pen. Easing himself underneath a rickety fence, he elbowed his mangled body through the agitated goats.

Somehow, he managed to manoeuvre around so that his back was leaning against a few supporting wooden slats. Blood pooled around him as lay slumped and semi-conscious.

The firing in the compound ceased.

Even the bleating of the goats subsided as an eerie silence descended upon the battleground.

Working on muscle-memory alone, Captain Anderson methodically re-loaded his M16.

Locked and loaded. Weapon at the ready.

His defiant eyes confirmed the inevitable. This was to be his last stand. 'Come on you fuckers,' he muttered.

The Captain's eyes blinked rapidly as he fought to remain conscious for the final act.

The night vision goggles were snapped into place. He was ready.

It wasn't long before he heard an Arabic voice whispering outside the goat pen. A turbaned head cautiously rose above the wooden gate.

The Captain fired. Crack! Crack! The head whipped back in a red mist and disappeared from view. One down. How many to go?

A grenade soared into the goat pen. Captain Anderson's eyes fluttered as he tried to focus on the revolving object. With an almost balletic grace, it seemed as if it was rotating in slow motion. It just kept hanging in the fucking air!

The grenade finally bounced into the middle of the pen, spun round and came to a rest at the Captain's feet. His broken body just couldn't react. His eyes shut as he waited for the pain. Only one word slipped out of his dying mouth. 'Hayley...'

The grenade exploded. Goats shrieked in agony. More shrapnel sliced into the Captain and his head slumped forward.

Four armed terrorists charged into the pen. The dying soldier somehow managed to unleash a final salvo from his M16. Two of his attackers were cut down. A third terrorist returned fire. The Captain's body jumped and twitched as the bullets hit home. He slowly slid down the wooden slats and came to rest on the blood-soaked ground.

Captain Anderson's killer turned to his surviving comrade and spoke in Arabic. 'Tell Khalid they are all dead.'

CHAPTER 15

Dawn. Aden seafront.

A single vehicle was parked on the edge of the harbour road.

Ahmed was in the driver's seat of his SUV, staring hypnotically through the grimy windscreen. Alone and on edge, he nervously tapped the steering wheel as he waited.

As the sun crept above the horizon, the passenger door opened. Ahmed flinched.

Colin Smith eased into the passenger seat, still wearing Arabic dress.

The visitor exuded a palpable menace as Ahmed continued to peer thorough the smeared glass. There was no initial eye contact between the two men. They both just sat in an uneasy silence.

Sweat dripped off Ahmed's strained face as he maintained his maritime vigil.

Smith dug a hand into his robe and whipped out a packet of cigarettes. Ahmed finally glanced across. 'You must not smoke in here,' he said quietly.

Smith smirked and lit up a fag regardless. He opened his window a concessionary few inches. 'That's the least of your fucking worries,' he said as he greedily sucked in the smoke and hacked out a rasping cough.

The two men remained mute for another minute. An unsettling calm before the storm.

The distant Muezzin's call to prayer softly infiltrated the confines of the SUV. That seemed to be the signal for Smith to speak again. 'It was very clear,' he said calmly. 'Move him. Keep him safe. No 'snuff' movies.' He took a long drag of his cancer stick and continued. 'Clear as crystal. Empty the compound. No welcome party or firework displays…'

Ahmed interrupted. 'I tried to tell him. To convince him.'

Smith ignored Ahmed's plea and continued. 'But what did we get? A decapitated hostage on film and 'Gunfight at the OK fucking Coral.' On the 'asset depletion' scale of one to ten it's a fucking eleven.'

'He didn't listen. I don't know, I just think he suspects something,' pleaded Ahmed.

Smith exploded. 'You don't know but you think that? I'll tell you what I think. I think that you're fucked. Fucked both ends.'

'It is difficult. These people are fanatics,' explained an increasingly agitated Ahmed.

Smith laughed and another cough spluttered out. 'Fanatics? Christ, they're no different from us. It's just that we don't wear pyjamas all the time. Simple matter of sartorial choice.'

He took a final puff from his dying fag then stuffed the burning remains out of the window. He pondered for a few moments then pulled a Glock handgun from his robe and started toying with it.

'However, it's your lucky day,' he said, turning to Ahmed. 'The Americans have got what they want, but my people need more. Yemen government targets. Who? What? Where? When? How? Calm your man down. Regain his trust. I need the Intel soon or they're going to cut you loose.'

'But they can't!' said a terrified Ahmed.

Smith rammed the Glock into Ahmed's temple. 'Not just you! Your family, your friends…your whole fucking world!'

Ahmed's head drooped forward in despair, his rigid hands now anchored to the steering wheel like a drowning man clutching on to a piece of driftwood.

Smith withdrew the gun. 'Don't want the bad boys taking an interest in that, do you?' He flung open the door and stepped out. After a short pause, he thrust his head back into the vehicle. 'I almost forgot,' he said grinning. 'The woman's become a liability. Tell your man to find her and kill her. Convince him that it's the will of Allah. A fanatic like him would appreciate that. I certainly do.' He slammed the door shut and strode away, his robe billowing in the stiffening sea breeze.

The warming rays of the morning sun began to filter into the SUV and illuminate Ahmed as he sobbed over the steering wheel.

***

Khalid slammed the Land Cruiser's door shut and trooped into the tower house with his men.

There was the usual tense silence in the rooftop kitchen as Quismah and Jalilah stood side-by-side preparing food. Their heads jerked up as Khalid swept in.

Nasir crept up the stairs and eavesdropped outside the kitchen door.

Jalilah rushed up to Khalid and spoke in Arabic. 'We have heard some news. Is it true, my husband?'

'God's will has been done,' replied Khalid.

Jalilah appeared flustered. 'This is not good. The soldiers will come and kill you.'

Quismah interrupted. 'My husband, you have done a great thing. Jalilah's faith is weak. God is great!'

Jalilah threw her husband a panicked look. 'The Americans will come for us all,' she bleated.

Khalid slapped Jalilah's face. She crumpled to the ground, wailing. He stared down at her with disgust. 'I cut the head off one Kaffir and you weep.'

'She has strayed from the Straight Path. She is lost,' declared Quismah.

Khalid screamed at Jalilah as she lay curled up on the floor. 'Prepare my food. I seek another infidel and must eat before I hunt her down.'

Crouched outside the kitchen, Nasir's eyes opened wide with fear as he heard Khalid's words. He scrambled down the stairs, rushed out the back and disappeared into the goat pen.

The panicked boy squatted down amidst the bleating goats and began to play his flute.

An inquisitive young girl climbed into the pen and sat down beside Nasir. He stopped playing and smiled at her. He leaned forward and whispered in her ear, 'Have you ever seen an angel?' The girl shook her head. 'I have,' he said proudly. 'She fell from the sky and was dashed on the rocks. But I found her and saved her.'

'Where is she?' the girl asked.

'She's safe. Hiding with my father in the mountains. I'm going to see her tomorrow and take her away so no one can find her and hurt her. Do you want to come?'

The little girl shook her head again, jumped up and skipped out the pen.

The girl raced through the village towards her mud-brick home. She dashed through the doorway and bumped into her father. He was a large bearded man in a billowing robe. An ammunition vest strapped around his chest marked him out as one of Khalid's men.

'What are you running from?' he asked his daughter.

The little girl hesitated. He gave her a stern look. 'Nasir has saved an angel,' she said.

CHAPTER 16

Charly and the leper sat in a tense silence around the blazing campfire. They hadn't spoken about Charly's nightmare and the leper could tell his angel was becoming increasingly agitated and remote.

The leper picked up some Qat leaves and slipped them under the cloth covering his face. He started to chew then offered some leaves to Charly. She ignored him and just gazed into the flames.

Gradually, the hallucinogenic properties of the masticated leaves began to take their effect. The leper's thoughts began to sharpen and crystallize. He gazed at Charly like a child staring up at the stars of a tar-black sky. There was beauty there, he reflected. No doubt about that. But also distance. Light years of distance. Protecting the essence of something that was unknowable and unreachable. Maybe that's why Charly reminded him of his wife. How can you love something so much, he thought, and yet know nothing about it? Faith. That was it. Faith is love. His wife and child were dead and his God had rejected him. His faith had crashed and burned an eternity ago, like a blazing comet ploughing into an abandoned desert. Now he was an empty vessel; his heart shrivelled up, just like his decaying body. No belief. No faith. No love. Just a twisted shell formed out of an unending and bitter hatred. And yet. Hope. Right there. In front of him. An angel descended from heaven. Could it really be her?

Charly finally spoke but her eyes never left the flames. 'You never pray,' she said.

'I have no God,' he replied. The leper lifted a portion of cloth from his mouth and spat into the flames. Qat juice sizzled in the fire. 'And you?' he asked Charly.

She slowly shook her head. 'I only believe in what I can see... and hold.'

Charly glanced at the key around the leper's neck and then at the dagger strapped to his belly. It was time to make her move. She sprang to her feet. ' Give me your AK47. Now!' she demanded.

The leper stood and backed away from Charly. He could see the determination flaring in her eyes. He clutched the handle of his dagger. 'I thought the honey would make you well but I was wrong,' he said. Inhaling deeply, he continued. 'I know the man who has taken your brother. The one with the eye-patch.'

'How? How do you know him?' Charly screamed.

'He is my sister's husband. His name is Khalid.'

Charly edged closer to the leper, like a hunter staking her prey. 'Why didn't you tell me this?' she shouted.

'If he finds you, he will kill you.'

Charly lunged at the leper. He stepped back. She cried out then collapsed. The leper rushed to her. 'Charly!'

Charly jerked and twisted on the ground, foaming at the mouth, as a major epileptic fit racked her body.

The leper panicked, unsure of what to do. He tried to restrain her thrashing limbs but the violence of the seizure was too great. He could only stand helpless, watching in horror, as his angel's body continued to writhe uncontrollably on the unforgiving earth. It seemed as if the wrath of the God he had denied was finally being unleashed.

Charly's seizure eventually eased and her convulsed body relaxed.

The leper wept as he knelt beside his unconscious angel. Tidying her hair, he murmured to her in Arabic. 'Charly, my angel. What is wrong? Tell me what to do.'

He stared at her, desperate for some sign. Anything that would give him hope. He could hear the rasping breath slip from her gaping mouth so at least he knew she was alive.

Straining hard, he lifted Charly's limp body into his arms and carried it into the cave.

It was dusk when the leper re-emerged carrying a prayer mat. He spread it on the ground beside the well.

He raised a bucket of water from the spring and ritually cleansed his hands and feet. He knelt down and faced Mecca. Bowing his head forward until it touched the mat, he started to pray to Allah in Arabic. 'Lead us on the Straight Path, the path of those thou hast blessed,' he recited, 'not those whom thou art angry or thou hast curst. God is great! God is great!'

The prostrate leper remained in silent prayer for a few moments, like a supplicant returning to the fold. He could feel the presence of his dead wife and child filling his heart again. He was consumed with love for his only son, Nasir. And as he continued to pray for the life of his angel, a sense of peace and grace began to envelope his crumbling body.

Purified and redeemed, the leper struggled to his feet and hobbled back to the cave.

The leper squatted beside Charly's sleeping body and watched as her chest moved rhythmically up and down like a gentle ocean swell. Her convulsions were now tamed and becalmed. He was pleased to see that – like him – she seemed at peace.

As he maintained his devoted vigil, the leper began to sing softly in Arabic as tears trickled down from his coal-black eyes.

***

Mid-evening in London. The rush-hour had abated and only the occasional car or cyclist journeyed past the row of Georgian terraced houses.

Inside one of the affluent dwellings, William Milhouse and his wife, Bridget, lounged in separate armchairs. A huge flat screen TV incongruously dominated the conservatively-furnished living room.

Milhouse cradled a large glass of whisky as he closely followed the news on the expansive TV screen. With obsessive precision, Bridget delicately worked a needle and thread through a piece of ivory-coloured lace.

Milhouse leaned forward as a male newscaster delivered the breaking news on TV. 'An al-Qaeda affiliated terrorist group in the Yemen, called 'The Arabian Islamic Army of God', has just posted the filmed execution of a British doctor on the Internet. Dr Ben Stevens was kidnapped eleven days ago in the Hadhramaut region of Yemen. The whereabouts of his sister, Charlotte – a senior manager working for Carrington Trust Petroleum – is currently unknown, although British government sources have indicated that they do not believe she is being held by the group responsible for her brother's death.'

Milhouse drained his whisky glass. His shocked face continued to focus on the TV as the newscaster continued. 'The terrorist group has also broadcast film of the mutilated bodies of four alleged British Special Forces soldiers. The Ministry of Defence has refused to comment.'

Still clutching his empty whisky glass, Milhouse grabbed the TV remote with his other hand and killed the TV. The remote fell out of his shaking hand and clattered onto the hardwood floor.

Bridget glanced up from her needlepoint. 'Terrible news. But what on earth were they doing there in the first place?'

'Humanitarian aid,' said Milhouse, glowering at his wife.

A patronizing smile stretched across Bridget's face. 'I'm sorry, dear, but you just can't help these people. But at least this has deflected attention away from your oil spill.'

Milhouse slammed his empty glass down on a side table. 'This was never meant to happen,' he shouted. He sprang up from his leather armchair and stormed out the room.

Bridget seemed puzzled. She shouted after her husband, 'What do you mean, dear?'

Milhouse staggered into a white antiseptic bathroom. He dropped to his knees and vomited into the pristine toilet bowl.

Clutching the wooden toilet seat with one hand, and the white-tiled wall with another, he dragged himself up. Bending over the sink he stared into the huge mirror. Tears filled his bloodshot eyes and rippled down his blanched, guilt-ridden face. It was as if a reservoir of emotion had fractured within his quivering body.

He grabbed a pair of manicure scissors and started to gouge the flesh of his left palm with the glistening blades. Blood pebble-dashed the alabaster sink.

He leaned his forehead against the mirror and began to sob, his body heaving like a ship in a storm.

A light knock on the door was followed by Bridget's chirpy voice. 'Cup of tea, darling?'

CHAPTER 17

The sun rose over the goat pen at the back of Nasir's house.

The boy eased open the heavy rear door, tiptoed out of the house and hurried past the pen.

Khalid and a group of his men stood at the edge of the rooftop and watched Nasir as he ran away from the village. 'We will follow him. But don't be seen,' barked Khalid in Arabic.

Nasir scurried along the sandy terrain, oblivious that he was being followed. As the blazing sun ascended the sky, he began to perspire. He dragged his arm across his brow but didn't stop. There was no time.

Tracking Nasir's footprints in the sand, Khalid and his men jogged along in single file.

Nasir clambered up the volcanic rock slope towards his father's hidden cave. His pursuers followed close behind, careful not to be seen.

Morning had broken over the mountainside and shafts of light streamed through the mouth of the cave.

Charly lay on the ground covered with a blanket. She stirred, confused and groggy, and placed a hand to her throbbing temple. It felt as if a Juggernaut had driven back and forth over her body for a week. Her head pounded and her tongue seemed glued to the top of her parched mouth. She reached out for a water bottle and glugged down the reviving liquid.

Charly looked across at the leper. He was still asleep and breathing heavily.

She placed a hand on the front of her damp jeans. That's when she knew she'd pissed herself. She nodded as the fragmented memories started to form in her hazy mind. Another seizure. Maybe half a day ago. Not surprising given the absence of her medication.

It was another fifteen minutes before she felt ready to move again. Slowly and silently, she rose to her feet. With an unsteady shuffle, she inched towards the slumbering leper. Her eyes remained fixed on the key attached to the piece of twine around his neck.

She stood over the snoring leper, working out what to do next. Picking up a sharp-edged stone from the cave floor, she began to delicately cut through the twine.

The leper snorted and turned towards her. Charly froze. But he didn't wake.

She resumed cutting. Finally, the key was released.

Charly crouched over the long wooden box and inserted the key into the stiff padlock. She jiggled it for a few seconds and the lock sprung open. She carefully lifted the creaking lid and peered into the box.

The leper's AK47 and ammo mag lay on top. Charly lifted them out and placed them on the cave floor. She looked back into the box and saw a large rug. Edging it aside, she found a sniper's rifle and a pile of photographs. Charly placed the rifle beside the AK47 then collected the photographs.

Charly examined the first photograph. It was a portrait of a beautiful Arabic woman. 'Hala,' she whispered to herself.

Charly studied the second photograph. It revealed the same beautiful woman but now accompanied by a handsome Arabic man and a baby. She glanced across at the sleeping leper and smiled.

Charly flicked through a few more photographs; relations, friends, weddings. The usual family stuff.

Then she selected a photograph from the bottom of the pile. As Charly examined it, her face filled with horror. The despicable image began shaking in her hand. The photograph depicted four heavily armed men – lined up and squatting on the ground. Beards, camouflage jackets and turbans marked them out as Taliban warriors. Laid out in front of the beaming men were two dead British soldiers. Mutilated and covered in blood, they were clearly trophies of war.

Charly shook her head in disbelief. She peered closely at the repulsive image. One of the Taliban soldiers was holding a distinctive sniper's rifle. She glanced at the rifle on the cave floor. It was the same rifle. She squinted at the photograph. The sniper's face? She frantically compared it with the photograph of the man with the beautiful woman and baby. It was the same man. It was the leper.

Charly stared at her sleeping protector and her face filled with hate. She silently picked up both weapons from the floor and carried them out of the cave.

Charly stood outside the cave entrance. Her hair was now tied up in a bun. She checked the sniper rifle was loaded. Satisfied, she laid it on the ground. She then examined the firing mechanism of the AK47 and snapped in the ammo mag. Ready.

Charly aimed the gun at the mouth of the cave. 'You Taliban bastard! Get out here!' she screamed in English.

A few seconds later the groggy leper emerged into the sunlight.

'Stop!' shouted Charly.

The leper halted. 'My name is Salim,' he said.

'When is Khalid coming for me?' she demanded.

'I would never betray you, Charly,' the leper exclaimed. 'I knew it was you but I couldn't believe it. That scar, your hair, those eyes. The first time I saw you, I knew. Allah had brought you back to me.'

'What do you mean?' said a puzzled Charly.

The leper's eyes twitched as the memory flooded back. Charly emerging dazed from the smoke-filled remains of the Army Land Rover. Her blonde hair spilling out of a tight bun. That cheek ripped open and streaming blood. The telescopic sight aiming at Charly's chest. His trigger finger hovering but not squeezing. The leper remembered it all. How could he ever forget?

The leper blinked and he was back in the campsite. He pointed at the scar on Charly's cheek. 'Khalid gave you that,' he muttered.

'What?' she said, looking confused.

'He fired an RPG into your Land Rover. Then I shot the soldiers.'

'It was you!' said a stunned Charly.

She took aim. Ready to fire. Her whole body trembling with rage. The leper nodded, as if willing his angel to shoot.

'When my wife died, I no longer wanted to live,' he explained. 'I followed Khalid to Afghanistan on Jihad. We fought for the Taliban and killed many British and American soldiers. But I couldn't kill you. I could never kill you.'

'That's where you were infected. In Afghanistan. Wasn't it?' Charly screamed. 'You were fighting for Allah but he cursed you. You wanted to be a martyr and go to paradise but instead you became a fucking freak!'

'I only wanted to die,' the leper cried, slumping to his knees.

'But you didn't die! You killed my men and now your fucked-up raghead friend has kidnapped my brother.'

Charly marched up to the kneeling leper. She rammed the barrel of the AK47 hard against his covered head. Her trembling finger hovered over the trigger.

'Charly. Please do it. Please!' begged the leper.

At that moment, the sound of Nasir's flute wafted into the campsite.

'Father! Father!' Nasir called out in Arabic.

Charly lowered her weapon and turned in the direction of Nasir's voice.

Hidden from the campsite by a group of trees, Nasir continued to yell to his father. 'Khalid has killed an Englishman. He wants to kill the angel. I have to take her away.'

Charly screamed at Nasir in Arabic, 'You are lying! He's not dead. I'm coming to save him.'

'Angel, Khalid has killed him and he wants to kill you,' Nasir shouted back.

Charly crumpled to the ground as a Tsunami of emotion overwhelmed her. The AK47 slipped from her grasp and clattered to the ground. 'No! No! Ben! Oh God, no!' she howled in English.

The stunned leper rose to his feet. He watched his devastated angel as her strength and resolve drained away in a river of tears.

One of Khalid's men crept up behind Nasir and grabbed him. He cupped a hand over the struggling boy's mouth and dragged him back down the slope.

A second armed terrorist moved stealthily through the trees towards the campsite.

The leper hobbled to Charly. He placed a consoling hand on her shoulder as she wailed.

The terrorist crashed through the undergrowth into the campsite. He stopped and aimed his AK47 at Charly. She looked up but was paralyzed with grief. The leper dived in front of his angel, shielding her body.

The terrorist fired. The leper was hit in the chest but managed to grab his own AK47, twist round and return fire. The terrorist fell dead.

The leper limped rapidly through the trees. He knew Khalid was near. He could feel it.

Two more of Khalid's men charged up the slope. The leper's AK47 crackled and they fell.

As the leper peered down the slope, bullets ricocheted off the volcanic stones around his feet. He dived behind a large rock.

Khalid's voice boomed out in Arabic from lower down the slope, 'Salim! It has been a long time, my friend. I see your aim is still good. I have Nasir. All I want is the woman.' Taking cover behind a boulder, Khalid grabbed Nasir by the throat and slapped him hard. 'Speak to your father, you little dog. Tell him!' he barked.

A defiant Nasir screamed up to the leper. 'Father! Don't listen to Khalid. Keep the angel safe.'

Khalid and his men laughed. 'Your son thinks that the Kafir is an angel,' he shouted. 'I think Allah has cursed him too. Bring her to me at the village. You have until nightfall. Or Nasir dies.'

Khalid and his men cautiously retreated down the slope with the boy.

The leper staggered out of the trees towards the campsite. The AK47 slipped out of his limp hands. Charly watched as the leper stumbled then collapsed. She rushed to him and knelt down. His robe was saturated with blood.

'You've been hit,' she said. 'Lie still. I'm going to get help.'

Panting for breath, the leper slowly shook his head.

The small bird fluttered in the air then landed on the leper's seeping chest. He squinted at the bird, struggling to focus. 'My little friend. How are you today? I have no food for you,' he muttered.

The leper coughed violently. The bird flew off. Blood soaked through the cloth concealing his face.

'I've got to get a doctor,' Charly said urgently.

The leper slowly raised his claw-like hand and unwrapped the cloth covering his head. Charly's eyes widened with shock as she saw what had, up to now, been hidden from her. The leper's face had been replaced by – what seemed like – a grotesque mask of hardened rubber; his handsome features now transformed into clefts of ossified skin and putrid flesh.

The leper looked lovingly at Charly and smiled. It was the first time she had seen him smile and she wept.

Charly spoke as her trembling fingers gently caressed the leper's ravaged face. 'I'm sorry. I'm so sorry.'

The leper's voice was now very weak. 'No doctor, Charly,' he murmured, 'it is too late.' He fought for breath, then continued. 'Khalid has taken Nasir and will kill him tonight. You must find your people and ask them to save my son. He will be in the tall house in the village, beside the Mosque.' The leper grabbed Charly's arm. 'When Nasir is safe, will you look after him? He has no one else.'

'I promise,' said Charly.

'Give him my Jambiya,' the leper said. 'Tell him to be a good Moslem and follow the Straight Path. Tell him that I always loved him.'

Charly nodded as tears trickled down her cheeks. She laid her anguished head on the leper's chest. 'Don't go! Please don't leave me!' she begged.

Struggling to breathe, the leper stroked her golden hair. 'Angel. My angel. You have brought me back to Allah. You have sweetness in your heart. Now I must go to my wife.'

The leper's head slowly turned towards Mecca; his decayed face finally infused with eternal peace.

Charly watched as the final breath escaped from her friend's body and his head lolled to one side.

The little bird chirruped. Charly raised her head. Her eyes followed the tiny creature as it flew onto the leper's still chest and hopped up to his ravaged face. She leaned forward and tenderly kissed the leper's tumescent brow.

Charly stood and walked to the well. She drew a bucket of water from the spring and returned to the leper's corpse. She tore a piece of cloth from the leper's robe and immersed it in the water. She then ritually cleansed the leper's twisted hands and feet with the dripping cloth. After wringing the cloth out and immersing it again, she carefully washed the leper's deformed face.

Charly rested her head on the purified body of her dead companion. Closing her tear-filled eyes, she said her own silent prayer for the man who had saved her life.

After a moment of quiet reflection, she slowly rose to her feet and looked down at the leper. He looked peaceful. Her eyes glanced at the AK47 lying on the ground and her face hardened. A decision was made.

Thirty minutes had passed. Charly hovered over the leper's body. She was now wearing Arabic robes and a turban. The leper's dagger was strapped to her waist. A dead terrorist's ammunition vest enveloped her chest and she cradled the AK47 in her arms.

She squatted down and wedged the photograph of Hala into the leper's clawed hand. She covered his face with some cloth and recited a final goodbye. 'Salam Alaikum. Sleep well. With Allah's help, I will keep your son safe.'

Charly sprang to her feet, snapped back the cocking handle of the AK47 and marched out the campsite.

CHAPTER 18

It was two hours before Charly reached the perimeter of the village. She emerged from the darkness and stealthily infiltrated the settlement.

In the distance she could hear the sound of bleating goats and barking dogs. Dropping to her haunches, she carefully reconnoitred the poorly lit area. She soon identified the five storey tower house beside the Mosque. Two Land Cruisers parked outside. Armed sentry at the front door. Target confirmed.

Crouching low, Charly crept like a panther to the rear of Nasir's house. Shielded by the goat pen, she observed another sentry guarding the back door. His head was drooped with boredom as he puffed on a cigarette.

She carefully placed her AK47 on the ground, unsheathed the razor-sharp dagger and crawled on her belly through the darkness towards the sentry.

She was within five feet when a goat bleated. The startled sentry's head shot up and spun round in Charly's direction. He aimed his weapon. 'Who's there?' he shouted in Arabic.

Charly lay still. The sentry stepped towards her, his sandals now only inches away from her face. His agitated eyes darted about but in the pitch blackness he could see nothing.

The sentry eventually turned and walked back to the door.

Charly leapt to her feet and crept behind the unsuspecting terrorist. She wrenched his head back, covered his mouth and slit his throat.

The man struggled as the life drained out of his body. Charly continued to hold and cut until he fell limp into her arms. She eased his bloody corpse to the earth.

The muffled sounds of Arabic voices spilled out of a second storey window. Charly looked up and then across at the back door.

The hinges of the heavy metal door squeaked as she pushed it open. She entered the building and found herself in the gloom of a primitive stone corridor. Bags of grain, meat and fruits lay stored against the wall. The tradesman's entrance, she thought, as she edged her way towards the bottom of a steep, rough-hewn stone staircase.

The Arabic voices above were now getting louder.

Charly tiptoed up the stairs, weapon at the ready. She followed the sound of the voices and soon reached a half-open door on the second floor. Inside the room, men were talking in Arabic and laughing.

Charly checked both sides of the hallway. Clear. She inched around the door and peeked inside.

The room was largely unfurnished; just a few cushions lining the walls and a carpeted area in the centre. Four of Khalid's men sat cross-legged on the ground, AK47s resting on their laps. They were watching a shaky replay of Ben's execution on a laptop positioned by a wall.

From the doorway, Charly struggled to focus on the laptop's images. Then she heard Ben's voice. He was pleading for his life. 'Please don't do this. I beg you. I came to help your people. I am not a spy.'

Charly gawped in horror. The AK47 vibrated in her shaking hands as the reality of her brother's merciless execution hit home. Her eyes squinted towards the laptop screen and she caught the images of Khalid pulling out the butcher's knife and grabbing Ben's hair.

'This is when the Kafir shit himself,' shouted out one of the seated terrorists. His watching comrades cackled.

Tears flowed down Charly's enraged face. She steeled herself, gripping her weapon tightly, as the depraved spectacle unfolded.

On the laptop screen, Khalid was now sawing through Ben's throat. Charly could hear her beloved brother choking and gurgling as he died.

Then the final image. Khalid raising Ben's decapitated head and screaming into the camera, 'Behold! This is the fate of all Crusaders and Infidels.'

Charly crashed through the door. Her AK47 thundered in vengeance. A long burst. RAT-A-TAT-A-TAT-A-TAT. Her body juddered with the powerful recoil.

The sustained hail of fire ripped into the unsuspecting men. They all jerked like marionettes as the bullets slammed into their bodies in a visceral explosion of blood and brains.

The room transformed into a blood-soaked abattoir and the massacre was over in seconds.

The laptop continued to play. With her jaw clenched shut, Charly fired another burst. The computer shattered into pieces.

Khalid stood clutching an AK47 at the doorway of the rooftop kitchen. He carefully listened as the gunfire below subsided.

Jalilah cooked in silence, her hands shaking with terror.

Nasir sat with his back to a wall. Quismah squatted beside him, holding a knife to his chest.

Khalid turned to Jalilah. 'Salim has come for Nasir. You guard the boy.' He glanced at Quismah. 'Go down to your brother. Tell him if he has not brought the woman then Nasir will die. Kill him if you can.'

'No!' screamed Nasir.

'Shut up!' barked Khalid.

Jalilah reluctantly walked over to Quismah, took the knife and squatted beside Nasir.

Quismah stood. She grabbed an AK47 from a table and headed for the stairs without speaking a word.

Charly marched out of the room and into the hallway. The acrid scent of gunfire hung in the air and she coughed. Her face was still contorted with rage as she reloaded her weapon.

Charly's head jerked up as she heard the sound of footsteps running up the stairs. She dropped to one knee and aimed the AK47 along the corridor.

The front door sentry reached the top of the stairs. He angled his AK47 around the wall with one hand and blindly fired. The bullets zipped over Charly's head.

The terrorist crept into the hallway. Charly's AK47 boomed. The bullets slammed into the man's chest and he slumped dead to the floor.

Charly edged along the hallway to the foot of the next set of stone stairs. She peeked round. No one. She slowly climbed up the steps.

Khalid stood ready at the kitchen doorway with his AK47. Jalilah held the knife to Nasir's throat but seemed distracted and kept staring across at her husband. Nasir took his chance. He sank his teeth into Jalilah's hand. She screamed. Nasir broke free and sprinted across the rooftop. Khalid spun round and fired at the fleeing boy. The bullets missed and Nasir vaulted over the edge of the roof. Khalid glowered at Jalilah then rushed to the roof edge. He looked over but saw nothing but darkness. Nasir had disappeared.

Charly was half-way up the stairs. Quismah appeared at the top step. Charly glanced up but had no time to react. Quismah fired. A bullet ricocheted off Charly's AK47. It jerked out of her hand and clattered down the stairs. The impact forced Charly back and she tumbled violently down the stone steps. Quismah ran after Charly, still firing.

At the bottom of the stairs, Charly rolled away as bullets thudded into the wall above her head. Quismah reached the bottom step. Charly grabbed her ankle and yanked hard. Quismah dropped her AK47 as she fell.

The two women viciously grappled on the floor; punching, kicking, gouging. Quismah shrieked with rage and compressed her powerful hands around Charly's neck. Charly was choking. Her bulging eyes rolled into her head as Quismah's vice-like grip continued to throttle the life from her.

Charly patted her hand around the floor, frantically searching for her gun, as Quismah continued to squeeze. Charly's fingertips located the AK47 but she was almost unconscious. With one final, desperate effort she head butted Quismah in the face. The stunned woman's head snapped back and bounced off a wall. Charly grabbed the weapon, rammed the barrel into Quismah's stomach and fired. Quismah groaned then went limp.

Charly struggled to her feet, clutching her bruised windpipe and fighting for breath.

After thirty seconds she had reloaded both weapons. Slinging Quismah's AK47 over her shoulder, she grabbed her own gun and hauled herself up the stairs.

Charly cautiously advanced along the fourth floor hallway. A voice shouted in Arabic from the rooftop, 'Salim is that you? Why are you doing this?' It was Khalid.

'Salim is outside with his sniper rifle,' Charly replied in Arabic. 'All your men are dead. The woman too. Now you are going to die.'

'Are you the Englishwoman?' asked Khalid.

'Yes,' Charly screamed back.

'I think Nasir may have been right. You ARE an angel,' Khalid said in fluent English.

The two deadly enemies continued to shout back and forth to each other.

'Your English is good,' complimented Charly.

'I studied as an Engineer in America.'

'And you fought in Afghanistan. You fired an RPG into my Land Rover and killed my men.'

This surprised Khalid. He paused for a few moments. Then the memory flooded back. 'I remember now,' he said. 'You are the crazy woman with the machine gun.' He grinned. 'Are you here to take my other eye?'

'No. I want you to see me when I kill you.'

Khalid laughed. 'So you are sending me to paradise?'

'You're not going paradise,' Charly hollered. 'You're going to hell.'

'Then I will see you there. Come. I am waiting.'

As Charly prepared for her final assault, she heard another Arabic voice – a boy's voice – at the end of the hallway.

'Angel. You have come for me,' said Nasir.

Charly wheeled round and saw Nasir standing by a window. 'Nasir?'

'I climbed down from the rooftop. It is easy for me.' He ran up to Charly and hugged her.

'Give me a gun. I will kill Khalid for you.'

Charly took the AK47 from her shoulder and handed it to the boy. She held her index finger up. 'On the roof. One minute. Don't fall,' she whispered in Arabic.

Nasir nodded and slung the AK47 around his tiny body. Weighed down by the leaden weapon, he lumbered to the window and clambered out.

Charly's eyes flickered as she checked her watch. She staggered, struggling to regain her balance. 'Not now!' she muttered to herself. She shook her head free of the sensation threatening to engulf her then rushed up to the rooftop.

Jalilah squatted against a wall, quivering with fear. Khalid stood aiming his AK47 at the kitchen doorway. He cocked his weapon as he heard footsteps pounding up the stairs.

Charly darted through the doorway, firing from the hip. Khalid was hit in the shoulder but managed to return fire. Charly's head jerked back as a bullet struck her temple. She crumpled to the floor. 'You are no angel,' Khalid screamed as he prepared to fire for the final time.

A voice cried out from the rooftop edge. 'Khalid!'

Khalid swivelled round and saw Nasir aiming his AK47. 'You little dog,' he snarled.

A dazed Charly scrambled about the floor, blood streaming from her grazed head. Still on her back, she grabbed her gun and aimed it up at Khalid.

Khalid turned back and saw Charly. He knew it was over. 'Allahu Akbar!' he shouted defiantly.

Nasir and Charly fired simultaneously. The sound was deafening as the two AK47s spat their bullets into Khalid. His riddled body slumped to the floor.

As the smoke of gunfire drifted into the clear night sky there was silence, broken only by the distant barking of a dog.

Jalilah cowered, snivelling, in a corner. Her hands covered her face in a desperate attempt to block out the carnage.

Nasir ran to Charly and hugged her. 'You are safe my angel.'

Tears of relief flowed down Charly's blood-caked cheeks as she stroked Nasir's bushy black hair.

'Is my father with you?' asked Nasir.

'No,' she replied in Arabic. 'He is with your mother now.' Nasir buried his head into Charly's chest and sobbed. 'We have to go,' she said.

Charly bent down and rifled through Khalid's jacket. She stole a set of keys then picked up her AK47. She grabbed Nasir's arm and hauled him out the doorway.

Jalilah crawled along the floor to her husband's contorted body. She slumped over the corpse and beat her fists into his bloody chest. 'My husband! My husband!' she wailed.

Through her tears, she spotted Khalid's discarded AK47. She scrambled to her feet, picked the weapon up and ran to the front of the rooftop.

Charly and Nasir rushed out the front door. A crowd had gathered. Some armed. Charly waved her AK47 wildly about. 'Get back! Now! Or I will kill you all!' she yelled in Arabic. The frightened villagers moved back

Jalilah leaned over the edge of the rooftop. She spotted Charly and Nasir running towards the first Land Cruiser. Balancing the AK47 over the edge, she pointed the barrel downwards. Her trembling finger prepared to squeeze the trigger.

Charly opened the passenger door of the Land Cruiser and bundled Nasir in. She ran around the front of the vehicle towards the driver's door.

On the roof, Jalilah had Charly in her sights. The AK47 started to shake in her hands. She blinked. Then fired.

Bullets thudded into the Cruiser's roof and pierced the ground around Charly's feet. Charly wrenched open the driver's door and dived in. She fumbled with the key in the ignition, desperate to start the engine. It clicked. Nothing.

Jalilah tucked the AK47 into her shoulder, ready to shoot again. She aimed the gun barrel at the section of the roof over Charly's seat.

Charly turned the key again. Another click. The engine roared into life. She floored the accelerator. The rear wheels spun in the dirt. Bullets peppered the back of the Cruiser as it sped away in a cloud of dust.

Jalilah fired again from the rooftop at the fleeing vehicle. Bullets ricocheted off the bumper as the fleeing vehicle disappeared into the darkness.

The murmuring crowd assembled again outside the tower house. A few seconds later, a body slammed into the dirt. The crowd circled the broken corpse. It was Jalilah.

As the Land Cruiser sped through the night, Charly glanced across at Nasir and smiled. The boy grinned back. 'Put your seatbelt on,' she said.

CHAPTER 19

The homeless seller proffered his magazines to sour-faced Londoners as they bustled past in contemptuous silence.

Annie, the Med-Team International worker, stood silently on the Canary Wharf pavement. She was carrying a brick. Looming over her was the enormous Carrington Trust Petroleum building.

She glanced at the CCTV camera swivelling towards her then raised her arm. She hesitated for a moment. The homeless seller stopped his hawking and stood, bemused, watching the lady with the brick.

Annie hurled the missile at a huge window. The pane smashed and shards of glass showered onto the pavement like iced confetti.

The homeless seller grinned at Annie. 'Nice one. Bunch of mean bastards anyway,' he said.

Annie sprinted off. Security men raced out of the building and took chase.

The homeless seller leaned against a wall, rolled up a fag and smiled as he enjoyed the fleeting victory.

An almost catatonic William Milhouse stood staring out of his expansive office window. He leaned his bandaged hand against the window pane. Blood from the seeping wound smeared across his own reflection in the glass. He didn't notice. His sad eyes just gazed through the sunny skyline - as if observing another, much darker, world.

Milhouse's landline rang. He flinched, then turned and walked to his desk. His hand hovered over the persistent phone, but he didn't pick up. The ringing stopped.

He slid on his coat, lifted his briefcase and quit the office.

The smeared blood slowly congealed on the glass.

***

Armed Yemen soldiers maintained a perimeter guard around the leper's campsite.

An Arabic figure of quiet and charismatic authority stared down at the leper's body. He was immaculately dressed in a Western business suit. The man was Jamal. Although now older, he was still recognizable as the Taliban soldier who had helped Salim drag Khalid to safety in Afghanistan.

He folded his hands on his breast and recited an Arabic farewell to his friend. 'Peace and blessings of God be unto you,' he said as a single tear rippled down his melancholy face.

Jamal bent down and dislodged the photograph Charly had placed in Salim's stiff hand. He peered at it, smiled, then slid the photograph back between his friend's twisted fingers.

An hour later, one of the soldiers sprinkled the remnants of earth from a shovel onto the leper's makeshift grave. He patted the mound flat.

The small bird flew down from a tree and landed on the grave. It chirped. Jamal glanced at the bird with a wry grin. He then nodded towards the soldiers. 'The village,' he said.

***

A convoy of Yemen Army Land Cruisers trundled into Nasir's village. The vehicles slid to a halt in a plume of dust.

Curious men, women and children emerged from their mud-brick houses and observed in an uneasy silence. They were the same villagers who had watched Charly and Nasir escape the night before.

Jamal stepped out of the lead vehicle. Armed soldiers followed in his wake.

Nine bodies, shrouded in white cloth, lay arrayed in front of Nasir's house.

The wizened village elder approached Jamal. 'God's peace be upon you,' he said.

'And God's peace be upon you,' Jamal replied.

The elder glanced at the corpses. 'O God, whoever You keep alive, keep him alive in Islam, and whoever You cause to die, cause him to die with faith.'

'Which one is Khalid?' enquired Jamal.

The elder pointed to the line of bodies. 'He is there.'

Jamal took a water bottle from one of the soldiers. He sprinkled the water over his hands then air-dried the skin with a waving motion. He started to check the bodies.

Jamal inspected the first three corpses with no success. He bent over the fourth body and gently pulled aside the shroud. He stared down at Khalid's rigid face, still fierce and intolerant, even in death.

Jamal glanced across at the elder. 'Who killed him?'

'The yellow-haired angel,' the elder replied. 'She was sent by Allah, may He be Glorified and Exalted.'

'Did she have a scar on her face?'

'Of course. She was a warrior,' said the smiling elder. 'And she took the boy with her.'

Jamal looked puzzled. 'The boy?'

'Nasir. The leper's son.'

***

London Wine Bar. Lunchtime.

Frederick Archer sat alone at a table. A laptop, a plate of Sushi and a glass of white wine lay before him.

He placed a piece of raw fish into his mouth with a pair of chopsticks then took an elegant sip of wine. His attention was focused on the laptop as it broadcast the latest news. A female newscaster spoke to camera. 'Here is some breaking news. In response to the globally broadcast execution of the kidnapped British doctor, Ben Stevens, the President of Yemen has just sanctioned the use of American hunter-killer drones within his country's airspace. It is thought that these drones will target key members of the Yemen-based terrorist group, 'The Arabian Islamic Army of God'. Western security agencies believe that this militant group is closely affiliated with al-Qaeda.'

Archer smiled and snapped shut his laptop. He leaned back and enjoyed another sip of wine.

Twenty minutes later, Archer was striding along the South Bank of the Thames. He carried a briefcase in one hand and an umbrella in the other. A self-satisfied grin was plastered across his superior face.

His mobile phone rang.

Archer stopped and hooked the handle of the umbrella over a railing. He placed his briefcase on the ground. A gloved hand drew the phone from his overcoat pocket. He pressed it to his ear.

'Speaking,' Archer said into the phone.

There was a pause.

'Excellent news,' Archer replied. 'Please pass on my congratulations to the American ambassador.'

Another pause.

'Not at all. Always a pleasure.'

A further pause.

'Yes. Nearly done. Just a minor matter to clear up.'

Archer listened for a few seconds, leaning against the railing and watching the Thames rush past.

'No. No.' he said into the phone. 'Simply a spot of housekeeping. Keeping it clean and tidy.' He nodded. 'Of course. I will. I will indeed.' He smiled. 'And you too. Goodbye.'

Archer removed the SIM card from the phone, dropped it onto the pavement and crushed it underfoot.

He lobbed the phone into the surging river and unhooked his brolly from the railing. Picking up his briefcase, he marched off.

CHAPTER 20

Aden.

A clear blue sky was draped over the sweltering and congested city.

The Yemen flag fluttered imperiously over a modern government building. A dusty taxi drew up and deposited Charly and Nasir outside the entrance. They walked hand-in-hand up to the armed sentries guarding the main door.

One sentry thrust his hand forward, gesturing for Charly to stop. 'Papers?' he demanded in Arabic.

Charly handed him a letter. 'We have an appointment.'

The scowling soldier waved the pair through the automatic door.

Inside, another guard swiped a hand-held metal detector over their bodies then waved them into the main building.

Charly and Nasir sat and waited for thirty minutes in the chilly air-conditioned reception area. A taciturn Arabic man approached and beckoned with his hand for the pair to follow him. He led Charly and Nasir through the palatial interior into a long corridor. He opened the door of a small room off the corridor and pointed in silence to two seats in front of a desk. Charly and Nasir entered and sat in the seats. The man left without speaking.

Charly grasped Nasir's hand and smiled. The boy embraced her hand and grinned back.

A minute later the door opened.

A small, mean looking Yemeni official entered and swaggered to his desk. He wore a sour expression and a crumpled suit. He sat facing Charly and Nasir. A uniformed soldier stepped into the room and guarded the door.

The Yemen official stared hard at his two guests. First at Charly. Then at Nasir. His sole intention was to intimidate and Charly could sense that this was going to be an interrogation rather than an interview. She shifted anxiously in her seat. Something didn't feel right and her fists started to clench.

The staring contest continued. Fed up with the official's bullshit, Charly decided to speak first. 'Have you the transit papers?' she asked in Arabic.

The menacing official ignored Charly and focussed his unwelcome attention onto Nasir. 'You little dog!' he shouted. 'Why do you want to leave Yemen with this Infidel?'

Nasir trembled in silence. 'Why? Answer me or I will whip you!' the official screamed.

Charly glared at the ranting bully. 'Leave the boy alone. If you have a problem then it is with me,' she shouted.

The official battered his fist on the table. 'Shut your mouth!' He jumped to his feet and scuttled like a crab around the desk. He hovered over Charly. She looked up, defiant as ever. This enraged him more. 'You come to our country. Kill our people. Kidnap our children. Then you think that you will leave here alive?'

'You need a man with a gun to protect you from a woman and a boy,' Charly said, smirking. 'I think you are a coward.'

The incensed official wrenched the AK47 from the surprised guard and forced the muzzle against Charly's head. A hysterical Nasir screamed out.

'You have just made your last mistake,' roared the official.

Charly grabbed the barrel of the gun, sprang from her seat and head-butted the scrawny man. He fell back, bounced off the wall and crumpled unconscious to the floor.

Charly swivelled round and pointed the gun at the guard. He instantly threw his hands in the air.

The door burst open and Jamal strode in. Charly pivoted round and threatened him with the AK47.

Jamal smiled and dipped his hand into his jacket pocket.

'Don't move!' screamed Charly.

Jamal calmly replied in excellent English, 'I have Nasir's transit papers. You are both free to leave Yemen.'

'You're a liar!' Charly shouted back.

Using two fingers, Jamal carefully and very slowly slid out a document from his jacket and threw it onto the floor in front of Charly.

Keeping her eyes on Jamal, she bent down and retrieved the document. Her eyes flitted back and forth, between the document, Jamal and the puzzled guard.

'See,' said Jamal. 'It is true. You and Nasir are safe. If we wanted to kill you, you would already be dead.' His eyes glanced down at the unconscious official. 'Forgive my overzealous friend. He was not authorized to speak with you.' Jamal kept smiling. 'Now please put the gun down and sit. I must speak with you now.'

Charly cautiously sat down. She laid the AK47 at her feet. Jamal stared at the guard and motioned with his head towards the official sprawled on the floor. The guard quickly dragged the insensible man out of the room.

Jamal threw Charly a cheeky grin. 'You ARE a crazy woman.'

Charly remained tense and suspicious.

'I know you speak Arabic,' said Jamal, 'but Nasir has no need to hear this so I will continue in English.'

Charly nodded, then turned to Nasir and gave him a reassuring smile. 'We can leave Yemen. This man is helping us,' she said in Arabic. A calmer Nasir grinned back. Charly turned towards Jamal. 'Say what you have to say.'

Jamal pulled the chair from the front of the desk and positioned it beside Charly. He sat and began. 'William Milhouse and a Yemeni national called Ahmed al-Hamali both work for Carrington Trust Petroleum…'

Charly interrupted. 'I know this. They are work colleagues.'

'But you don't know that they also work for your country's MI6.'

'Don't be ridiculous!' said Charly, shaking her head.

Jamal was unfazed and continued. 'MI6 organized the kidnap of you and your brother. They used Khalid but could not control him. Your brother's execution was not part of their plan.'

'Their plan?' Charly shouted. 'What are you fucking talking about?'

Jamal paused for a second, allowing Charly to calm down, then continued. 'My country's oil will run out soon but our neighbours in the Gulf have plenty. They fear that if Islamic militants fight Jihad in Yemen then the entire Arabian Peninsula will fall into chaos. Their paymasters in the West agree. Both the Americans and the British have been putting pressure on the Yemeni government to crack down on local militants. They have also pressed our President to sanction American drone missile attacks in Yemeni airspace.'

'What has all that got to do with my brother's kidnap and murder?' said a puzzled-looking Charly.

'It was the perfect excuse they needed to exert additional pressure on my government. And it worked.' Jamal pulled a US dollar bill from his jacket pocket and held it in front of Charly. 'For some people in my government, this is the only thing that has value. A Yemeni life is like a grain of sand in the desert. Worthless. However, a Westerner's life? That is significant. That will get the required reaction.' He crumpled the bill and threw it onto the floor. Nasir scrambled from his seat and grabbed it. 'But times are changing,' said Jamal. 'My people are starting to see the snakes slithering around their feet.'

'Why should I trust you?' asked Charly.

'Because the leper was my friend.'

'You knew Salim?'

'We fought together in Afghanistan for four years. He saved my life. That's why you have been allowed to take Nasir to England. I am repaying a debt.'

'You work for your pro-Western government and yet you are a Jihadist?'

Jamal smiled. 'You come to Yemen with a Medical Aid programme and yet you are a Crusader. We are the same, you and I. We both fight for our own worlds in our own ways.'

Charly was silent as she digested what Jamal had just said. It made sense and she knew he was right. Deep down, she just knew.

After a minute of contemplation she asked the one question she had never been able to ask the leper. 'How did Salim become infected?'

'American bombs destroyed a leper village. We were all scared to help them. Apart from Salim. He went in. Saved many children, but...', Jamal paused briefly, '...a year later he disappeared. I never saw him again but I heard he had returned to Yemen and was living alone in the mountains as a leper. He was a good man. The best I have ever known.'

Charly slowly nodded. It was strange, she thought; the leper had changed both their lives but he was dead and here they both were – united by the one man who had given them a common cause and transformed their mutual hatred into some kind of acceptance. It felt confusing and yet, at the same time, strangely comforting.

'What do you want from me?' Charly finally asked Jamal.

'Your brother was a guest in our country. I believe he truly wanted to help our children. His death was unjust and has dishonoured our people. Our law decrees that if you want revenge then you can take it.'

'I've had enough of killing,' said an exhausted Charly.

'I understand. Khalid is dead. But the men who are truly responsible for your brother's slaughter are still alive. Milhouse and Ahmed will make more trouble for you and Nasir. I can deal with them. You don't have to say a word. Just nod your head and it is done.'

Charly's haunted eyes stared at Jamal. He could see death inhabited her, as if ghosts from the past were present in every wrinkle and crease of her anguished face.

Her head remained still as she gazed across at Nasir. The boy was closely scrutinizing the crumpled dollar bill. He was the future and she smiled. It was time to end it, she thought, to finally let go. So she slowly shook her head.

Jamal smiled. Part of him had hoped Charly's heart would prevail. 'Your mercy is stronger than your wrath,' he said. 'It is God's will. Peace be upon you.' He rose from his seat and looked at Nasir. 'Keep on the Straight Path,' he told the boy in Arabic. 'May Allah open the way for you.'

'May he make you strong,' Nasir replied, smiling at the mysterious stranger.

'All of us together, 'Jamal said, placing the palm of his hand over his chest. He walked to the door and halted. He turned and looked at Charly. 'The people in Salim's village are happy that Khalid is dead. They talk about you. They call you the 'leper's angel'. In Islam, angels are sacred. Make sure the boy prays. Allah will do the rest.'

Charly nodded. Jamal opened the door and left.

CHAPTER 21

Ahmed pushed his father's wheelchair along the scorching Aden seafront promenade. His young son scampered beside the wheelchair holding his grandfather's bony hand.

A voice cried out, 'Ahmed!'

Recognising the voice, Ahmed stopped and his eyes clenched shut. His young son looked up and caught his father's distress.

Colin Smith ambled up, puffing on an unfiltered cigarette and still wearing Arabic dress. He smiled at the boy. 'I must speak with your father for a moment. Is that OK?' he said in Arabic. The confused boy nodded.

Smith grabbed Ahmed's arm and dragged him towards the sea wall. Waves crashed against the white concrete barrier and covered the two men in a spray of salt and foam. Smith chucked his damp fag into the churning wash.

'There are some things you can't avoid in this life,' Smith said. Ahmed remained mute. Smith glanced across at the boy. 'Happy families. You're a lucky man, Ahmed.'

'Why are you doing this to me?' asked a weary Ahmed.

'Because you failed. And because I can.'

'I did everything that was asked of me.'

'You certainly did. And look where we are now.'

'But it's finished!' Ahmed pleaded.

'It's never finished,' said Smith with a twisted smile. He tapped the dagger resting on Ahmed's belly. 'You're sharp. You know that.'

The boy observed the men with rising concern. He could feel his father's visceral fear.

Ahmed had had enough. 'My father is sick. I must go,' he said walking away.

The petrified boy watched as Smith wrenched his father back by the arm. The boy sobbed and hugged his unresponsive grandfather for reassurance.

Smith jabbed his finger into Ahmed's portly stomach. 'Don't walk away. Do not ever fucking walk away from me again,' he snarled. 'I'm the only one keeping you alive.' He stared hard into Ahmed's terrified eyes and smirked. 'Ironic, isn't it? I'm the only friend you've got in this Godforsaken world.'

Ahmed glanced towards his weeping son. Desperate to end this living nightmare, he turned back to Smith. 'What do you want me to do?'

Smith pinched Ahmed's cheek with mock affection. 'That's better.' He handed Ahmed a piece of paper. 'That's where they're staying. That's when they're leaving. All you have to do is give confirmation on the ground. Nothing more than that.'

Ahmed took a quick look at the paper and reluctantly nodded.

Smith continued. 'Our friends will contact you. Make sure you're ready. No more mistakes…,' he looked across at the boy, '…or innocent people may get hurt.'

Ahmed's head flopped down in despair, as if the tendons in his neck had been severed.

Smith ambled up to Ahmed's son. The fearful boy reared back. Smith ruffled the sobbing child's bushy hair then strolled off.

As the distraught boy wailed, the catatonic grandfather sat motionless in his wheelchair - his lifeless eyes fixed on the distance, as if staring into a gaping black abyss.

***

The isolated U.S. Predator Drone Base was located deep in the Saudi Arabian desert; a secret hidden world of lethal Western technology with no other discernible sign of life.

Anonymous buildings punctuated the sandy lunar-like landscape.

Formidable security fencing surrounded three large clamshell-style hangars.

Two long 'hard surface' runways stretched into the shimmering distance.

A huge satellite dish, twenty feet wide, marked the epicentre of this UAV Ground Control Station.

When it seemed that nothing or nobody was moving in the baking midday heat, a hangar door slowly opened and disgorged a strange looking flying machine. It resembled an enormous metallic insect.

The RQ-11 Predator drone rolled silently onto the runway as if powered by its own malevolent volition. A five-foot long AG-114 Hellfire missile was fixed to the beast's undercarriage. This was no pleasure craft.

The unmanned drone accelerated along the runway and rose inaudibly into the sky like an avenging angel of death. It soon became a dot in the cloudless blue expanse.

A CIA Operations room in Langley, Virginia, controlled the drone. It was filled with high-tech tools designed to rain down death and destruction onto the doomed and unwary.

In a sterile low light, an impassive CIA technician in a crisply ironed cotton shirt sat surrounded by banks of screens and state-of-the-art computer equipment.

Muffled intercom chatter wafted around the clinical laboratory-like space.

A large screen was positioned directly in front of the technician. He wore a headset and his hand gently manipulated a small joystick as he peered into the screen.

The Predator's 900mm lens swivelled round as it captured a high altitude image of the barren desert landscape.

'UAV airborne,' the technician said into his headset. 'All systems go. ETA to target four hours.'

***

Ahmed's SUV was parked near the front of a Western-style hotel. He sat alone in the driver's seat and observed the entrance. Placing a mobile phone to his ear he relayed the current status in English. 'They are still in the hotel.'

Charly stood in her hotel room and packed a suitcase lying on a double bed. Nasir sat on the other side of the bed playing his flute. She stretched across, patted his head and smiled. 'I need to phone someone. Then we will go and fly in a plane,' she said quietly in Arabic.

Charly rummaged around the suitcase and brought out a model of a passenger jet. She handed it to Nasir. He grinned with delight as he flew the plane around his head, making whooshing noises as it banked and dived in the air.

Charly fanned her face with her hand in an effort to cool down. She walked to the window and threw open the wooden shutters. A small bee buzzed into the room.

She lifted an archaic phone from the bedside table but hesitated. The bee darted around the room as Charly closed her eyes and took a deep breath. Finally, she dialled and pressed the receiver to her ear as she nervously listened to the dialling tone.

There was click on the other end of the line as the call was answered. A frail elderly female voice with a Manchester accent spoke. 'Hello?' Charly's body started to shake. She struggled to reply but the words just wouldn't form in her mouth.

The fragile voice on the other end of the line persisted. 'Hello? Who is this?'

Charly moved the receiver back towards the hook. Her trembling hand hovered, ready to hang up. She looked across at Nasir. He was still gleefully sweeping the model plane through the air. He glanced back and smiled.

The bee landed on the table beside the phone and slowly crawled around. Charly stared down at the little insect. A wistful smile crept across her sad face. As her tear-filled eyes followed the tiny creature, she whispered to herself. 'Sweetness.'

Charly urgently thrust the phone back up to her ear and blurted into the mouthpiece, 'Hello.'

'Do you have the wrong number?' said the elderly lady. 'Can I help you?'

'My name is Charlotte Stevens.'

'Yes dear. What is it?'

Charly's voice started to fracture but she eventually said it. 'I'm…I'm your daughter.'

Ahmed continued to observe the hotel.

At the entrance, a local taxi driver smoked beside his battered car as he waited for his passengers.

Charly and Nasir walked out of the hotel. Ahmed leaned forward in his seat as he watched Charly hand her suitcase to the taxi driver. She and Nasir climbed into the back of the taxi. The driver threw the suitcase into the crumpled boot then mumbled something into his mobile phone. He then jumped into the driver's seat.

As the taxi drove off, Ahmed spoke into his phone. 'They have left in a taxi. I think they are heading for the airport. I will follow for visual confirmation.'

The SUV accelerated away in pursuit of the taxi.

Charly's taxi bumped along the rutted tarmac road at high speed. Ahmed's SUV followed close behind.

At an altitude of fifteen thousand feet, the Predator drone cruised in the cloudless sky above Aden. The drone's 900mm lens swivelled then locked on to Charly's taxi and Ahmed's SUV. Both vehicles were now being tracked from the sky.

The taxi driver spoke in Arabic into his phone as he trundled along the pot-holed tarmac. 'I'll be back from the airport in thirty minutes.'

In the CIA Operations room in Langley, the drone technician peered at his computer screen. He could see the Predator's zoom lens stalking both vehicles as they raced through the Aden suburbs. 'Target's mobile phone signal confirmed. Locked on,' he said calmly into his headset.

As Nasir played with his model plane in the rear of the taxi, he intermittently checked the creased dollar bill still clenched in his hand. Charly looked across and gave him a reassuring smile.

Ahmed's SUV roared along the road following the taxi. As he flashed past a large white Mosque, the amplified voice of the Muezzin floated into the car's cabin. Ahmed's taut face relaxed slightly as he heard the mellifluous call to prayer.

In the taxi, Nasir thrust his plane down with a noisy whoosh.

The CIA technician in Langley pressed a button. 'Launch confirmed,' he announced into the headset.

The Hellfire missile launched from the drone's undercarriage with a whoosh.

Moments later, there was an enormous explosion and the taxi's rear window shattered. Reacting to the blast, Charly grabbed Nasir and shielded him with her body.

The taxi driver slammed on his brakes. The taxi slewed to a halt in the dust beside a large warehouse.

Charly frantically twisted round in her seat and peered through the demolished back window. She could see in the distance an orange ball of flames incinerating Ahmed's SUV. A huge plume of black smoke billowed up from the mangled wreckage.

'Get out now! Take cover!' Charly screamed in Arabic to the driver.

The panicked man jumped out and sprinted away.

Charly battled to open the rear door of the taxi but it was stuck. She punched and hammered on metal and glass but it wouldn't budge.

She braced herself for the impact of another missile strike. A direct hit this time, for sure. But it didn't come.

With one final powerful kick she eventually managed to break open the jammed door. She jumped out and hauled Nasir from the back seat.

Charly and Nasir raced for their lives towards the large warehouse at the side of the road. Confused Arabic workers stared as the pair dashed inside. Charly stopped and hugged Nasir tightly.

'OK?' she asked.

'OK, Charly,' said Nasir grinning.

The boy wrapped his arms around his angel's waist.

The crumpled dollar bill fell from his hand and bounced off the sandy floor.

CHAPTER 22

London's morning 'rush hour' traffic streamed along the elegant Georgian street.

William Milhouse stood in the hallway of his terraced house. His heavily-bandaged hand clutched a briefcase. With a distant look he called to his wife. 'See you tonight.'

Bridget appeared from the kitchen. She sensed her husband's detachment. 'You are alright William, aren't you?' she asked.

'I'm fine,' he lied.

'It's just that you've looked a bit peeky recently. A bit 'off'.'

'Just tired of this Yemen thing,' he said, forcing a smile. 'Nearly over.'

Bridget returned the smile but was not convinced. She adjusted her husband's collar then wiped some thread from the shoulder of his coat. Housekeeping and attention to sartorial details were the ways in which she expressed her affection.

'You're a good man, William,' she said.

'Am I?'

'Of course you are! Got your sandwiches?'

Milhouse patted his briefcase. Bridget pecked him on the cheek. 'See you tonight, dear.'

He nodded, opened the front door and left.

Frederick Archer sat alone on a bench in St James's Park. The handle of his umbrella was hooked over the arm rest and a mobile phone was already positioned to his ear. He didn't like being made to wait by anyone and his impatient fingers drummed on his hand-made silk trousers.

William Milhouse approached the bench and sat down beside Archer. Leaving the usual privacy gap, he took his phone out. It was the same drill as before. Two strangers who happened to be sitting on the same bench.

'You're late,' snapped Archer.

'Board meeting.'

'Of course, silly me. How is your oil spill?'

'Officially plugged,' confirmed Milhouse.

'And unofficially?' asked Archer. He briefly glanced at Milhouse's bandaged hand. 'Stigmata?' he suggested.

'What?' said a puzzled Milhouse.

'The hand. Stigmata?'

'Pruning,' said Milhouse.

'Excision. A necessary evil. Got to get rid of that dead wood.'

'Is that why you killed Ahmed?'

With jaunty indignation, Archer replied. 'Not me, my dear boy! Cowboys across the pond. Now that they have the green light to recommence their remote-controlled 'activities' they seemed keen to tie up that particular loose end. You know how trigger-happy they are.'

'He was only doing what he was ordered to do,' exclaimed Milhouse.

'Of course. Of course he was. You and I both know that. But if one bats for both sides one's bound to be bowled out sooner or later. Odds of the game, I'm afraid.'

'Am I a loose end?' asked Milhouse.

'Good God man, we're not savages,' protested Archer. ' We look after our own.' He paused. 'I think that you and Bridget…that is her name, Bridget?' Milhouse nodded abruptly. Archer continued. 'I think that you and Bridget need to take a well-earned rest. I hear the West coast of Ireland can be quite invigorating at this time of year. Especially if you get the weather.'

'And Charlotte Stevens?' queried Milhouse.

'Ah, yes,' said Archer, smiling. 'Charlotte of Arabia. Quite a woman. Word is that she's gone native on us. Just like her bloody predecessor, Lawrence. I wonder if she owns a motorbike? Seems the type.'

'She's an epileptic.'

'Is she indeed? Even better.' Archer paused again, taking time to reflect. 'Anyway,' he said, 'apparently she's bringing home an Arabic boy. One more won't make any difference. I hear the London Mosques are quite spacious.' His face filled with a condescending smile. 'Actually, we're rather hoping he'll join the Club when he's older. Always a quota to fill now that the lunatics have taken over the asylum.'

A bee buzzed around Archer's head. He tried to wave it away with an irritated swipe of his mobile phone. The bee landed on the bench and fanned its tiny wings.

Archer surreptitiously unhooked his umbrella from the arm rest and aimed the wooden handle at the insect. The handle clattered down onto a slat. The unscathed bee flew off with an extended zzzhhh.

'It would appear that I have lost my touch. Happens to us all, I suppose,' said Archer pointedly.

'So that's it?' said Milhouse, shaking his head.

Archer slowly rose to his feet. 'Yes. That's it,' he replied. 'Must dash. Got some of my own pruning to do.' With that parting shot, Archer slid the phone back into his jacket and swaggered off. He twirled his umbrella and whistled "La ci darem la mano" as he went.

Milhouse remained seated and watched as Archer melted into the promenading crowds. 'Arsehole,' he muttered to himself, as he opened his briefcase and took out a shrink-wrapped sandwich and a small bottle of hand gel. He washed his hands with the gel then unwrapped his lunch. Taking a bite of his sandwich, he stared across the path at a blooming flowerbed and carefully observed a cluster of bees as they hovered over the plants and collected their life-giving pollen. His mood lifted and he smiled, the first time in a long time.

Milhouse finished chewing then made a call on his phone.

An apparently innocuous helmeted cyclist strolled along the path wheeling his bike. Just another London commuter. He headed towards Milhouse's bench.

'Bridget?' Milhouse said into his phone. 'Fancy a holiday?'

The cyclist stopped in front of Milhouse. It was Colin Smith. He looked down.

Sensing Smith's looming presence, Milhouse glanced up. 'Can I help you?' he said with a puzzled look.

'William?' said Smith.

'Do I know you?' asked Milhouse.

Smith smiled then slid his hand into his jacket and pulled out a handgun fitted with a silencer.

Phat! Phat! Phat! Three bullets slammed into Milhouse's chest.

Phat! Phat! Two into the brain.

Smith calmly mounted his bike and cycled away.

Milhouse's bloody corpse slid off the bench and crumpled onto the path.

A woman screamed. A passer-by ran up to help. A crowd gathered.

The assassin's bicycle faded into the distance as the bees continued to harvest their pollen.

ABOUT THE AUTHOR

Gary Mill is a Scottish writer of novels, screenplays and songs. He currently features on the BBC's 'Writers List'. His first seven e-books have appeared in (and topped) a number of Amazon Top-100 'fiction' charts: *Action/Adventure*, *War*, *Mystery Thriller*, *Scottish Crime*, *Conspiracy Thrillers*, *Historical Fiction*, *Urban* and *Dark Comedy*. Gary is currently working on his eighth book and all his novels are now available in paperback.

Other e-books written by GARY MILL

'THE LEPER AND THE ANGEL' - published February, 2014.

This high-octane thriller is set in the Arabian Peninsula. It tells the story of Charly (Charlotte) Stevens - an embittered Afghanistan war veteran - who forges an unlikely friendship with a reclusive leper as she battles to evade the clutches of murderous terrorists and free her kidnapped brother. But not everything is as it seems. Charly is unaware that her real enemy lies hidden in the shadows. As events build to a shocking and bloody climax, she discovers a revelation which will change her life forever.

Customer reviews (an average of 4.7 out of 5 stars)

"This book keeps you reading, and is exciting and well written." ✫ ✫ ✫ ✫ ✫

"The storyline is very compelling and sometimes quite visceral...the unrelenting pace made for an exciting read." ✫ ✫ ✫ ✫ ✫

"Another great read by this author. The plot and setting were different to the other books so I was wondering how it would unfold. Similar style of writing, easy to pick up and return to. Most enjoyable." ✫ ✫ ✫ ✫ ✫

"Excellent story, well written, good book." ✫ ✫ ✫ ✫

"This was very intense reading. The characters were well developed and the story held my attention...I couldn't put the book down...I would recommend it to anyone who likes a book that grabs your mind and holds your attention to the very end." ✫ ✫ ✫ ✫

'BLACKFRIAR' - published May, 2014.

'Blackfriar' is a contemporary, neo-gothic murder mystery set in Edinburgh. Laced with black humour, it tells the atmospheric tale of Chrissie Dewar - a strong but embittered ex-Catholic police detective - who is struggling to find her missing sister, catch a serial killer, and salvage her abandoned faith. As the spectre of a black-hooded killer looms large on the streets of Scotland's capital - and the legend of the Blackfriar ghost permeates the sinister subterranean vaults of the 'Old Town' - Chrissie embarks on a blood-soaked journey into the heart of darkness. What she discovers there will test her courage, and fragile faith, to breaking point.

Customer reviews (an average of 4.5 out of 5 stars)

"Very enjoyable, with lots of twists and turns...the cast of characters were excellently drawn." ☆ ☆ ☆ ☆ ☆

"Highly recommended." ☆ ☆ ☆ ☆ ☆

"A good tale which held my interest." ☆ ☆ ☆ ☆ ☆

"Blackfriar keeps an entertaining pace and is packed with memorable characters. I'd recommend this book to those who like their humour black and their killing creative." ☆ ☆ ☆ ☆ ☆

"Really enjoyed this book: interesting characters and a good plot that kept me wanting to read more. Just about the right length for me, and the way the story unfolded kept me interested from start to finish." ☆ ☆ ☆ ☆ ☆

"Great read, let yourself go and buy into the plotlines. You will enjoy it. Some fabulous characters, tons of twists and turns and a goodly lodge of humour. Get reading it now, you will not regret it." ☆ ☆ ☆ ☆ ☆

"Creepy and twisty in equal parts. Loved it." ☆ ☆ ☆ ☆

"A great read, plot moved along quickly and held together well. I thoroughly enjoyed it." ☆ ☆ ☆ ☆

"Good story. I live in Edinburgh and found the history and descriptions accurate and interesting. Overall, an enjoyable read." ☆ ☆ ☆ ☆

"Recommended as a quick read to pass a few hours and both light-hearted and realistic enough to immerse your mind. I did hear the characters in my head with a thick Edinburgh accent which added to the enjoyment." ✩ ✩ ✩ ✩

"Enjoyed this. It kept me thinking." ✩ ✩ ✩

'SASKIA'S SOLDIER' – published January, 2015.
'Saskia's Soldier' is the first novel in the 'Jock Mackinlay' series. It contains two stories (or episodes).
Episode 1 ('Saskia's Soldier') is a mystery thriller with a twist set in Holland. It follows Jock Mackinlay - a traumatised and alcoholic ex-army veteran of the Falklands War - as he travels to The Hague to hunt down the secretive killers of his estranged son. It's the redemptive tale of a damaged Scottish soldier's struggle to confront his demons as he discovers it's never too late to find the courage to change and make things right.
Episode 2 ('Vessels of Liberty') is a pacy thriller set in Edinburgh and Perthshire. Jock has dried out and is now leading a settled life. But his world is turned upside down when he investigates the suicide of an old comrade. He is soon ensnared in a duplicitous web of intrigue when some of the most powerful men in Scotland take lethal steps to prevent him from revealing their diabolic secret.

Customer reviews (an average of 5 out of 5 stars)

"A masterpiece! I read this two-part thriller after downloading Gary Mill's 'Parcel of Rogues' for free on Amazon – therefore out of sequence, but this in no way detracted from the storyline (Hey! It worked for Star Wars and it most definitely worked here!) This is a wonderfully crafted piece of work which I highly recommend to lovers of authentic crime thrillers." ✩ ✩ ✩ ✩ ✩

"Bone-crunching action, sleazy antagonists and a unique anti-hero of the Scottish variety. Another thoroughly enjoyable read." ✩ ✩ ✩ ✩ ✩

"Not being a regular reader, this book kept me reading until it was finished. – which is a good thing! So good, I went on to read Book 2 in the series ('Parcel of Rogues'). Hope there's more coming from this author." ✩ ✩ ✩ ✩ ✩

"Excellent story in two parts. Worked really well. Loved the association with Edinburgh throughout. Looking forward to the next one." ★ ★ ★ ★ ★

'PARCEL OF ROGUES' – published June, 2015.

'Parcel of Rogues' is the second novel in the 'Jock Mackinlay' series (part 1 – 'Saskia's Soldier' – was published on Amazon Kindle in January, 2015). Edinburgh, 2014. Scotland votes against independence in the referendum. The news is greeted by a massive and devastating explosion outside the Scottish Parliament building. The tartan terrorists are back, after a hiatus of nearly twenty years.

The Alba Liberation Army terrorised the UK in the early 1990s, bombing and assassinating without compunction; until one man infiltrated the group and stopped them - Jock Mackinlay, ex-special forces MI5 undercover officer. After the terrorists were apprehended and jailed, Jock melted back into the shadows.

Now Jock's returned, recalled from extended 'sick-leave' by the machiavellian MI5 chief, John Cairnville. Back on the booze and with his granddaughter on life-support after a hit-and-run car crash, Jock's not in a good place but Cairnville's desperate and his fragile foot soldier is the only card he has left to play.

Cairnville teams Jock up with Karen Miller. One of the new MI5 breed, she's professional, well-trained and extremely adept at surveillance techniques. Miller doesn't initially bond with the grizzled dinosaur but the fireworks really begin when the brash, super-confident Inspector Jamie Fraser from Special Branch enters the mix. Jock and the younger man embark on a long-term pissing contest which threatens to destabilise the investigation.

As Jock's past returns to haunt him, and his life goes into meltdown, the terrorists and their horrifying objective are finally identified. Jock, Miller and Fraser converge on the target for a decisive confrontation with their ferocious adversaries; a brutal encounter which will claim lives on both sides.

Customer reviews (an average of 4 out of 5 stars)

"Utterly brilliant! Excuse my language but this book was s**t hot. I read it in one sitting and was totally bowled over. The story line is captivating and the characters are 'up in your face'. The authenticity of this novel is amazing and is a terrorist thriller of immense substance. A must-read for the lover of gritty, dirty, deceitful practices of the secret services." ✰ ✰ ✰ ✰ ✰

"This author's style of writing makes it easy to picture the main characters in the book and the story kept moving fast. I'm not looking for books that take an age to read and this book was easy to read over two days. Most enjoyable while reading on holiday next to the pool.' ✰ ✰ ✰ ✰ ✰

'MY GOOD LADY' – published February, 2016.
'My Good Lady' is the dramatised account of a true story.
It is 1914. The staid, morally righteous and male-dominated Victorian era has given way to a potentially more liberal Edwardian period. However, women remain second-class citizens and still do not have the vote. Britain's menfolk have gone to war but the female population must remain behind and keep the home fires burning. After all, the fairer sex don't fight; that is not their role in life. But one iron-willed female doctor from Edinburgh has a very different idea; an idea borne out of political struggle and a steely determination to succeed. Her name is Dr Elsie Maud Inglis.
A founder member of the Suffragist movement in Scotland, Elsie stirs her fellow activists into action. Ensuring financial independence through an extensive and successful fund-raising campaign, she establishes an exclusively female medical relief organisation: The Scottish Women's Hospitals for Foreign Service. Elsie's 'girls' are an ill-assorted bunch from a variety of backgrounds but they share one thing in common – an independence of mind which refuses to be cowed by accepted social convention and the repressive political status quo. Yes, Elsie's volunteers will wear uniforms and go to war. But they are an army of a different kind; an army of medical pioneers engaged in a perilous battle to do their duty and win their freedom.
Elsie and her team of female doctors, nurses, orderlies and drivers soon travel to war-torn Serbia, Russia and Romania and find themselves in a hellish crucible of war. Forced to fight against the extreme weather, diabolical living conditions, horrific injuries, virulent disease, constant bombardments and deep-seated personal conflicts they start to wilt under the relentless pressure. Despite everything, the SWH women find the courage they thought they didn't

have; the will to go on they suspected they did not possess; and the hope for peace they believed could never be achieved again. At the beginning of the "great adventure" Elsie tells her girls, 'if you do your utmost then you will be victorious'. In the face of overwhelming odds and perpetual conflict, each woman finds her own way to battle through and achieve a personal victory – a victory of which their inspirational leader would be proud, but one which would exact a great personal cost.

The stirring tale of Elsie and the SWH is fascinating, exciting, inspirational and profoundly moving. It is the story of courageous women exposing themselves to the greatest of dangers so that lives could be saved and men could be healed. It is a story of selfless sacrifice which should never be forgotten.

Customer reviews (an average of 5 out of 5 stars)

"Brilliant." ☆ ☆ ☆ ☆ ☆

'TAM'S THE MAN' – published September, 2016

Tam Stewart is a circus fan: he's a juggler, tightrope walker and one of the hardest c**** to have ever pounded the pot-holed promenades of Sighthill since he was knee-high to a Rottweiler. Tam has been mentored by Joe Mackenzie, Wester Hailes' foremost drugs baron, and most fully committed psychopath (Joe's affectionate nickname is 'Mack the Knife' - say no more). Now that Joe is "on his way oot" due to a spot of cancer, it's time for Tam to step up to the plate and take over the reins of power. Trouble is, Tam is a sensitive soul and - despite an impressive history of extreme violence, chronic larceny and unabated drug-dealing - he has no desire to inherit Joe's evil crown. Plus, he's just fallen in love with Anna, a beautiful emigre from Poland. Tam's solution to this seemingly intractable problem is to carry out one last massive drug heist, without Joe's consent. Then he's out. Out for good. To amble into the sunset, hand-in-hand, with his true love.

What could possibly go wrong?

WARNING!

If you are the type of person who is offended by bad language and scenes of gratuitous sex and violence, fear not. Although most of the dialogue is in the "earthy" Edinburgh vernacular, it is as pure as the driven f***** snow; and there are only a few instances of explicit sexual acts and blood-drenched brutality (no more than you would normally witness on a Saturday night in Edinburgh's Lothian Road).

If you like your humour jet-black, and enjoyed Martin McDonagh's "In Bruges", then you'll love "Tam's the Man".

Or you won't.

It's up tae f****** you, pal. Know what I mean, eh?

'FLODDEN' – published May, 2017

On Friday 9th September 1513, a battle is fought on the wet, windswept slopes of a Northumbrian hill. The armies of Scotland and England have clashed on countless occasions before, but never on such a savage and merciless scale. *Flodden* tells the story of this barbaric conflict and of the fates of two Scottish men whose destinies collide on the blood-drenched killing ground: James IV, King of Scotland, and Fletcher, a young arrow maker from Selkirk. As both men become immersed in a horrific and inescapable cauldron of violence, they desperately fight to remain alive and keep their souls unsullied. But in this most brutal of fights to the death, only their God will know who will live and who will die.

23996864R00072

Printed in Great Britain
by Amazon